Tied for Murder

Percy Peacock, psychologist, who used his gifts to unravel the dark skeins of mystery in *Death Rings a Bell*, the previous Fitzsimmons whodunit, appears again in the present one where his talents are even more desperately needed. In the high school of Palos Rojas, California, where the local First Aid class met under the direction of Gloria Smead, the entangled lives of a debonair husband and a betrayed wife create both a sensation and a dilemma. That death should enter where people devoted themselves to the art of preserving life was incongruous but tragically inevitable. The "victim" in one of the first-aid demonstrations, neatly bound, was killed when an ill-timed blackout gave the murderer his chance. The problem of Percy Peacock was rendered more difficult and complicated because the town of Palos Rojas was full of people who bore the insoucient but unfortunate victim deep lying grudges. With his usual skill, Cortland Fitzsimmons leads the reader through the maze of suspicion and antagonism to the unexpected solution.

By the same author:

DEATH RINGS A BELL
THE EVIL MEN DO
ONE MAN'S POISON
SUDDEN SILENCE
THE MOVING FINGER
DEATH ON THE DIAMOND

By Cortland Fitzsimmons and Gerald Adams:
THIS—IS MURDER

Tied for Murder

BY
CORTLAND
FITZSIMMONS

A
MYSTERY
NOVEL

WILDSIDE PRESS

www.wildsidepress.com

I

IT WAS A clear evening. Across the channel Catalina Island loomed large and rugged, her mountains etched with burnished light. A warm rose-gold tinted the town of Palos Rojos. It caught on sea-turned windows and flashed back toward the west. The gold lost its brilliance. The rose grew deeper until the sea and sky were brushed with dark brooding red.

Percy Peacock was in his garden marveling at the riotous sunset over the Pacific when the telephone rang. For a moment he pretended not to hear it. The last call had had unpleasant overtones. It had been Christopher Smead telling him in rude tones to leave Gloria's mind alone. Christopher's cool nerve, his assumption of authority over his ex-wife had exasperated Percy to the point of telling Christopher to mind his own business. He had deliberately returned the receiver to the hook.

Trying to ignore the commanding tone of the bell, he stood watching the rapidly spreading red as he made an effort to reassemble his thoughts. What was going on beyond the sunset's glow? What of Japan—how much she had done in so short a time out there beyond the horizon. What part would he ultimately play in the long struggle which lay ahead?

The bell continued to ring. Automatically he had counted the peals. There had been five. Most casual callers stopped after that. He waited, counting six seven and eight. The tone was sharper. He shrugged in defeat. The frantic urgency of the ringing made thought impossible.—There was an insist-

5

ence in its shrill tones that pulled him toward the house. It was a local call, he felt sure of that.

"All right, all right! I'm coming," he called to the instrument as he entered the living-room.

He lifted the receiver and was about to resort to an old trick of pretending to be his Filipino house boy. He had saved himself many aimless conversations by this ruse but he realized that the trick would no longer work. Lonzo had enlisted in the early days of the war, anxious to get back to the Philippines to fight for his country.

Before he could utter a word Gloria's voice said accusingly, "Percy, where on earth were you? I was afraid I couldn't get you."

He was about to explain but she hurried on, "Come to the school tonight please. Take me home after the class. I need you, desperately."

He was going to ask her if she had told Christopher about his effort to help her with their marital problem, but he didn't have a chance. The line went suddenly and exasperatingly dead.

"Desperately!" he repeated. It was not like Gloria to be extravagant with her adverbs. She really meant it.

"Christopher is up to something again," he thought, "and she is afraid of herself."

He knew it was Christopher. It could be nothing else. It had always been Christopher with Gloria from the time they had first met. He knelt on the windowseat to look at the fading glory of the sunset and admitted that it would always be Christopher. He admitted it with regret, not because he had any but a friendly interest in Gloria and the fact that he had tried to help her. He had tried because she had asked for his assistance to free herself from the compulsion of Christopher.

The great red ball of the sun was squeezing itself between

sea and sky. About him the hills were washed in the red light. "Covered with the sun's blood," he mused.

He felt himself shiver. "Not blood," he said aloud and the words seemed to wipe out the threat from the sky. The glow faded quickly.

He lit a cigarette, thoughtfully watched the match flame until it crept dangerously close to his fingers. He puffed it out, realizing that he was thinking of death in connection with Christopher, death as a means of freeing Gloria from the man's hold over her.

"Quit it, Peacock," he said. "You know better. What would your classes think, what would the University say if they knew that you had premonitions, half believed in them like any old fishwife?"

Percy was a teacher of psychology in one of the Los Angeles universities and, while he thought he knew more than the average man about human nature and the workings of the human mind, he held no brief for himself about his knowledge of women. He knew that certain things should be true, understood the mental habits, of transfer and identification, knew about fixations and all that sort of thing, but he was afraid he had failed utterly in helping Gloria. She had asked for his help. They had talked. She had been as frank as a woman could be under the circumstances but she had not been able to get Christopher out of her system.

He had explained, had gone over case histories with her, had dwelt upon her hurt pride, her desire to be as all-inclusive to Christopher as he had been to her. Having a quick intelligence, she had seen all his points. She had agreed with him when he told her that Christopher had not changed, that the man she loved was the product of her imagination and not the man that Christopher really was and would always be. He had tried to make her see that she had taken an idea about Christopher and mentally had made him fit the pattern of the ideal, forgetting that Christopher was definitely his own man.

Christopher could not help being a philanderer any more than the wind could help blowing in from the sea every afternoon about three o'clock. Gloria had wanted him to be different, had hoped that she could make him over, had wanted him for herself and herself alone. Her hurt pride had brought about the divorce, and she had left Palos Rojos for nearly a year. Now she was back teaching the First Aid Classes at the evening highschool and Christopher had again entered her life.

Percy himself rather liked Christopher. He had no illusions about Christopher and took him for what he was. Christopher's was an engaging personality. He had a trick when talking to you of making you believe that you were the only person in the world. It was a flattering experience if you didn't understand the man. He was gracious, generous—often with your time and money—had a ready laugh that was infectious, and, Percy admitted, a magnetic charm for women.

Women had been the trouble in the past, the reason for the Smeads' divorce. Now Christopher had the nerve to tell him, Percy, to leave Gloria's mind alone. Gloria was not sure of herself, was afraid of what she might do, wanted Percy to be with her as a policeman to give her both mental and physical support. Percy was thoroughly aware of Gloria's self-division. Her body wanted Christopher while her intellect told her that she would never be happy with him again.

He knew there was nothing more that he could do but he was willing to be a physical prop if she thought it would be of any help. He regretted people's fooling themselves, their refusal to face facts, to see themselves as they were. But there was nothing he could do about it.

He decided to walk to the school. Without a car, he would have a legitimate excuse to ask Gloria to drive him home. He stood for a moment on his terrace absorbing the night smells. The sweetness of the large bed of nicotiana made him regret anew the necessity for going out.

He had plenty of time. He knew if he hurried he might intercept the police car at the foot of the hill and ride with his friend Bill Dunning until it was time to arrive at the school. Long before he reached the foot of the hill he saw the police car flash by. It was going in the direction of Redondo.

When he reached the road he stood for a moment to look at the tents of the unit which was encamped at the edge of the cliffs. Outlined against the fast darkening sky a sentry paced back and forth. Somewhere beyond the sentry there was a listening device to warn of the approach of planes.

He walked slowly. The windows of the school shone brightly, illuminating the plaza and the long flight of steps which led up to the building. Recess had not yet ended. People stood around the yard in clusters, smoking cigarettes and chatting.

At the base of the steps he ran into Christopher and Billings, who were talking intimately. He heard Christopher say. insolently, "Why should I? All is fair in love and war and we are at war, aren't we?"

Christopher flipped his cigarette into the air. It made a high arc and landed on top of one of the cars. He turned and started up the steps, grinning at Percy as he passed.

"Hey!" Billings called angrily, "that cigarette landed on my car and it has a canvas top."

"It'll roll off," Christopher replied with characteristic lack of regard for people or their property.

Billings hurried to his car and brushed the cigarette to the

pavement and ground it out with his heel. He looked up at
Percy and growled, "Why someone doesn't kill that rat I
don't know."

Dead-pan Billings, they called him in the community. He
was a large man, something over six feet, with a completely
expressionless face. He was senior warden of the district and
head of the local real estate concern which bore his name.
He had been part of the Palos Rojos community from the
beginning of its development in the boom days of the late
twenties. Insurance was one of his sidelines.

Billings' business had not been good after the Japanese
submarine scare along the coast. For a time it had seemed
that every other house in the Palos Rojos estates had had a
"For Sale" sign posted on its lawn. There were no buyers,
however. Except for the old established residents people in
general were not shore-minded. Some of the newer residents
moved away. Many of them said it was because of transportation; that their tires could not stand the many miles of driving
to and from town. The net result for Billings had been a
falling-off of most of his business.

Since Billings had been grumpy for weeks, Percy was not
surprised at his wrath against Christopher. He felt that Billings' annoyance at the carelessly thrown cigarette stub was
justified. Billings swore, "I'll get even with him if it's the
last thing I do, so help me, I will!"

There could be no doubt that the man was angry, yet
nothing in his face gave an inkling of his feelings. He fell in
step with Percy who had started the upward climb.

"Immoral, that's what he is," Billings announced as they
reached the top step.

"He's amoral," Percy corrected. "He has absolutely no
sense of right or wrong. No more morals than a sardine."

"Don't try to make excuses for him to me," Billings
grumbled.

Percy laughed. "I'm not. I was trying to explain him, his lack of ethics. He never had any, never will."

"Sounds crazy to me," Billings muttered. "People like that are not in their right senses."

"We say amoral morons for certain types," Percy added, "but Christopher isn't a moron—or is he?" he corrected himself. "I wouldn't be too sure. Perhaps we have been making a mistake and he is a true moron after all."

"Whatever you want to call him with your fancy language is all right with me, but he hadn't ought to be allowed around decent people," Billings complained.

"Maybe the army will get him," Percy suggested.

"No such luck. If you ask me, that's why he's trying to get Gloria to marry him again," Billings puffed.

"Is that the reason?" Percy asked.

"What else could there be? He treated her like dirt the first time, was glad to get away from her, wasn't he?"

"I don't know. I rather thought it was something else," Percy answered thoughtfully.

"What?"

"A safety motive."

"That's what I mean—so he won't have to go in the army."

"I wasn't thinking of that kind of safety. Marriage gives an immunity to men like Christopher. As long as they have wives they are, in a sense, protected from the women to whom they devote their away-from-home attentions."

"I won't argue with you. He thinks of himself first all the time, and you might be right." Billings ground his cigarette on the sill just outside the door. "I shouldn't be so mad," he said. He turned and entered the building.

Billings continued on up the stairs to the second floor and the classroom. Percy crossed the lobby to the drinking fountain, which was behind one of the flights of steps. The main staircase was split. There were two sets of steps going up from the lobby against the circular walls of the well which had been built for them. They met on a small platform on the second floor. Under one flight there was the drinking fountain—under the other a telephone booth. The area under the landing was not lighted. The rear door opening on the school garden in the center of the courtyard was open. The lights from the rooms above shed an uncertain glow over the outer courtyard.

As Percy drank at the fountain he heard voices just beyond the door.

It was Christopher pleading earnestly, "I know I've been a fool, Gloria. I know what a mess I made of our lives, what I did to you. If you would only believe me when I say I'm sorry, that I want to make amends to you for the rotten way I treated you! There has never been anyone but you, there never can be. You must know that in your heart. Say you'll forgive me. We could go away tonight, to Yuma or Las Vegas and be married and begin all over again."

They had been moving slowly toward the door. Percy was caught. He didn't want to appear to be eavesdropping, and yet he didn't want to let them know that he had heard. He bent over the fountain again.

"I so wanted us to be happy, Chris," Gloria said. In his mind's eye Percy could see the lovely earnestness of Gloria's deep blue gaze, the warm, sweet curve of her mouth as she breathed regrets for their broken marriage. "I could never understand why we were not. I tried to be everything to you—perhaps it was all my fault." Honest as always. Taking a blame which was not hers. Percy moved impatiently.

"No," Christopher denied emphatically. "You were perfect."

"I was jealous, will be again, if I come back to you . . ." she murmured tentatively.

"Oh, Lord!" Percy thought. "She's done for; she's giving in."

Christopher was quick to follow the advantage. "Come back to me," he begged.

"I warn you, Chris, the first time I learn that you have broken your promises I'll . . ."

"You'll never have to worry about that again," he said glibly.

There was silence. Percy moved away from the fountain to the lighted part of the lobby. Just beyond the door Gloria stood in Christopher's embrace. Percy groaned inwardly, but his mental comment was ironic. "So much for my efforts as a helper."

Henry Graham came along the corridor. He slowed down for a second and glanced out toward the garden. He turned and mounted the stairs slowly.

"A picture of complete dejection," Percy thought.

Henry must have seen the lovers. His narrow, dark head sagged forward, his thin shoulders drooped, his arms hung lifeless and his steps were as measured and slow as the steps of a man going to his doom.

"He must love her very much," Percy thought pityingly.

Gloria came through the door. Her face was radiant, her eyes filled with a happy light. She crossed the lobby and entered the principal's office. Christopher sauntered out from the shadows. While Gloria radiated happiness and the joy of living, Christopher gave Percy the impression that he was pleased with himself, smugly satisfied with his recent accomplishment. For a moment Percy hated the man, hated him for what he would do to Gloria, again and again.

There was no point in his staying at the school. Gloria had no need for him now. She had done the very thing she had been afraid of doing. Percy started for the entrance; he could go home to his pipe and his books. A woman stopped him to ask him a question on child psychology. Gloria came out of the office and moved toward them.

"Percy!" Her voice rippled with happiness. "Will you help me out?"

"But . . ." Percy was puzzled.

"I'm giving the class an examination. It is the last night. I'm short one person to make four teams. Will you be a judge for me, please?"

"If you really need me."

"I do. We'll be in room 212. I want to start in five minutes." She hurried away; ran lightly up the stairs.

He followed more sedately and was just a few steps behind her when he reached the second floor. He smiled to himself at her buoyancy. She seemed to float down the corridor. Suddenly she stopped as if she were frozen to one spot, completely bereft of animation.

Through an open door he saw why. Christopher was in a classroom with a slim, dark-haired woman in his arms. He was kissing her as if she were the only woman in the world. The woman was Ruth Teale. She clung to him hungrily. He could see the whiteness of her hand as it moved over Christopher's back, pressing his body closer to hers.

He saw Gloria's hand go up to her face, cover her mouth, saw the back of her hand pressed hard against her lips. Then her hand moved as if it were scrubbing her lips. Her arms fell to her side and she moved forward slowly at first. Gradually her pace increased until she finally broke into a frantic run toward her classroom.

The lovers' embrace was broken when Percy passed the second door. Christopher and Ruth Teale were moving from the room. Christopher grinned at him and winked with a you-understand-old-fellow nod of his head.

Percy continued on his way. He found Gloria at her desk,

her head bent forward over the papers which she was sorting into neat piles. He sat on a chair just inside the door and waited. When she looked up there was no indication of what she was feeling. She seemed to be her usual self. She even smiled at Christopher when he sauntered in, slid into his chair and favored her with a slightly intimate wink. His attitude, his eyes, the little hovering smile at the corners of his mouth seemed to say, "We have a secret, you and I."

"That look, more than anything he has done, would make me want to murder him," Percy decided indignantly.

Some such indignation seemed to take possession of Gloria as she faced the class and waited for the rustling of the members to subside. She was fighting hard to control herself. Percy saw the flesh on her arms quiver.

With a noticeable effort she began: "Now that recess is over, we shall take up the practical part of this examination. I want to know how much you have learned from this course. With Mr. Peacock there are twenty-four of us. He has kindly agreed to be one of our judges. We will have four teams of six members each. There will be four workers on each team, a victim and a judge. I will give the judge a list. He is to mark the team, taking off points for things which are done wrong, deducting points for slowness, lack of efficiency and speed. I don't want you to race through your problems but I want you to remember always that quickness often means the difference between life and death, particularly in cases of severe bleeding.

"I want the judges to note the things you do first. If you do not take care of the most important injury first you will lose points. The four workers will be graded on the basis of the judge's report. The victim on each team is to write a report of his impressions of the treatment he received. If he feels that the workers seemed inefficient he must say so.

"A wounded person is very sensitive and lack of efficiency

and bungling will discourage him, remember that! The victim will be graded by his report. The judges will be graded on the basis of their papers and the keenness of their observations. I will act as a general supervisor watching all teams, noting the things you do and how you do them so that I shall be able to check on all of you, judges, victims and workers alike. Each set of workers will have a captain who is to tell the other workers what to do while he works along with them. Is everything clear?"

There were one or two questions, which she covered quickly.

She went on with her instructions. "We will go to the cafeteria where a place has been cleared for the preliminary work. Each problem includes transportation, so I want the judges to watch carefully.

"Now about transportation. When you have finished your work your judge will tell you where to take your victim. When your victim has been properly transported to the proper place you are to follow your judge, who will take you to one of the other victims. You are to find that victim, check on the work done by the other team, make any corrections necessary to insure the safety and comfort of the victim and then bring him back here to this room. Our work will take us to various parts of the building but we are to return here to room 212 at the end. The team who arrives first and has the fewest marks against it will naturally have the best rating."

She read off the team groups and appointed judges and victims. "Remember," she cautioned again, "you must tell the judge what you are doing as you work."

Christopher was the victim on the team Percy was to judge. Ruth Teale, Benn Higgins, Alice Walker and Martin Brown were the workers.

When they assembled in the cafeteria the blankets were

spread on the floor and the victims took their places. Gloria gave each judge a tabulated marking sheet. Then she reversed a portable blackboard on which the problems were stated. She allowed them two minutes for reading the problem.

Percy's team's problem read:

A man has been blown from a building by an explosion.
He has a simple fracture of left leg below knee.
A compound fracture of upper right leg with severe arterial bleeding.
A scalp wound in center of head just above hair line.
A contused wound on left cheek.
He is unconscious.
After four minutes there is danger from a tottering wall.
The victim must be rescued from that danger.
Transport victim to room [244.]

The team members buzzed over their problems, lined up at the foot of their victims with their equipment ready. Gloria checked over the class, passed out slips of paper to the judges on which were written the number of the room to which the victim was to be transported and blew her whistle. The workers advanced on their victims with zeal.

Christopher was grinning as Ruth Teale started shock treatment at once. Higgins ran the palm of his hand up Christopher's leg and applied pressure at the groin. Christopher made a wise crack to Higgins who paid no attention. Percy deducted a point from the team.

While Higgins applied pressure, Brown applied a tourniquet on the upper right leg. He was fast and proficient. He marked Christopher's brow indicating tourniquet and time applied.

Ruth explained to Percy that she was applying heat. She put a blanket lightly over the left leg and covered as much of the body as she could.

Alice Walker went directly to the head and began work on the scalp wound, explaining to Percy that she was applying iodine, a sterile compress and a bandage. She dropped the compress. He deducted points for failure to be sterile when she picked up and used the fallen compress.

With the tourniquet in place and tightened, Higgins moved down, tested the pulse and then helped Brown dress the wound. The dressing in place, Higgins applied traction to the right leg. Brown adjusted the traction splint, took care of the traction with the ankle hitch, tied the splint securely, checked the tourniquet again and propped the splinted leg which Higgins released.

While they had been busy Ruth had examined Christopher's eyes, had raised his head slightly.

Alice and Ruth had then shifted to the left leg, stepping over the victim. Percy deducted points for that carelessness. Alice applied traction to the left leg while Ruth applied and tied the splint in place.

While the two women were finishing their splint, Higgins applied a hot pad to Christopher's stomach but failed to test it for degree of heat. Percy deducted more points. Higgins then covered the right side of the body with a blanket while Brown put a sterile dressing over the contused wound.

Their work done, they covered their victim and lifted him to a stretcher. Gloria passed by just then and bent down to look at the bandages on the head and cheek.

"Don't forget we will leave immediately after school," Christopher whispered, but they all heard it, even Percy, who was standing a few feet away.

"His hands should be tied if he is to be transported," Gloria said as she rose, giving no intimation that she had heard his remark.

Ruth Teale was kneeling beside Christopher but she showed

none of Gloria's composure. She tied Christopher's hands together, tied them viciously with a granny knot, pulled it so tight that Christopher complained.

The workers lifted the stretcher, forgot to relieve the head-man before the order to move was given. Percy deducted a point for that. When that error had been corrected he moved ahead of them out of the cafeteria.

At the door of his office stood Fred Hewing, the principal of the school. Well as Percy knew Fred, the principal's appearance never failed to give his categories a shake-up.

For there was none of the traditional mustiness of the schoolroom about Fred Hewing. He was handsome in a healthy, outdoors sort of way. He was six feet tall and had the straight, powerful shoulders, the sturdy slimness and easy grace of the athlete. An extraordinarily fine physical specimen as well as an able school executive, Fred Hewing had surely been favored by fortune.

Under the gaze of the principal Percy straightened his own shoulders, made resolution to start setting-up exercises and a rueful mental note to watch out for that stoop over his desk when he became absorbed in his work.

"Hi, Percy!" Hewing waved his hand to the little procession. Percy waved back and grinned. Commanding as his presence might be, Hewing was a genial individual whose cordiality endeared him to students and townspeople alike.

Christopher shouted from the stretcher, "Hey, Fred, look at how these people have me foul." Hewing smiled back broadly. In mock complaint Christopher grumbled something which Percy did not hear. Percy's attention had been diverted by pert, funny little Fanny Hayes who scurried up to him and asked, "Ooh, Mr. Peacock, hello there! Where is it that your team is bound for? Say, did you know that I—"

"Room 244," Percy interrupted succinctly and moved

away quickly. Fanny, though a cute little trick, could be an infernal nuisance unless one cut short her babble; and there was work to be done.

On the second floor he walked down the hall while the team followed with the stretcher. Percy opened a door which he thought was room 244. A scream of shock greeted him. He closed the door quickly on one of the funniest sights he had seen in a long time. Marjorie Blake was standing on a platform. She was three-quarters mummy and one-quarter woman. The upper part of her body from neck to hips was covered with wet clinging paper. Between the edge of the paper casing and the top of her stocking Percy was conscious of garters and white flesh.

Marjorie tried futilely to cover herself, pulling at the paper-casing in which she was enclosed. Percy hurriedly closed the door and Christopher joked, "Take me in there."

"She's having her form made," Alice explained as they went along the hall. "That was one of the fitting-rooms for the dressmaking class."

"Some form!" Christopher said with ardor.

They carried him into the room and deposited the stretcher on the floor. This room must be one of the manual training rooms, for as the side stretcher-bearers moved in, one of them jolted against some pieces of two-by-fours which were standing in the corner. The two-by-fours clattered and banged to the floor.

After Christopher had been safely deposited the pieces of lumber were put back in place.

"Now where do we go to check on the work done by the other team?" Higgins asked.

"The victim you are to check on and transport back to room 212 is in room 310," Percy replied and turned to the door.

They left Christopher and were in the center of the building, almost at the main stairway when Hewing, the principal, dashed up the steps and paused a moment to call excitedly, "There's a blackout. The lights will be turned off in a minute, the bell system isn't working. Warn the classes down the hall. I'll take the other end. Those of you who are wardens had better go to your posts." He raced away.

It was not until that moment that they heard the sirens. In the pause of shocked suspense which followed Hewing's announcement there was complete silence. The siren could be heard faintly and then a deeper horn boomed out from the plant at Redondo.

They scattered at once and were spreading the alarm when the lights went out.

II

THERE WAS GREAT commotion. The sound of excited voices mingled with nervous laughter and the rapid scurrying of feet. Fresh in the minds of all was the memory of the recent Los Angeles blackout accompanied by gunfire, which had blazed away in the middle of the night.

Over the flurry within the building Percy heard cars starting up and racing away. Wardens' whistles shrilled after the people who were breaking one of the first rules of blackouts, the driving of cars on the highway.

He knew they would soon be stopped, for Palos Rojos was almost a military zone and the army was in many and unexpected places.

An old lady bumped into him and squealed. She asked him in a quavering voice where she should go for safety. She had forgotten, as many of them had, that the auditorium had been equipped for blackout purposes. He took her frail arm and led her carefully to the top of the stairs, then guided her down to the door of the auditorium which was draped with heavy black curtains. He led her in, blinked at the sharpness of the lights and helped her into one of the rear seats.

"I'm not afraid, really," she said looking up at him. "It's—well—it's always so sudden. It is upsetting, because we never know, isn't it?"

He agreed with her and went back to the darkness of the hall. People were milling about in the lobby. He could make out dark shapes crowding toward the door, jostling one another. Mrs. Billings lumbered down the stairs, crossed in front of him. In the dark she looked enormous.

He went to the front door and watched the shore line. The lights of Manhattan Beach and Hermosa were out. Redondo suddenly went black. In the direction of Hollywood and Los Angeles there were bright spots in the sky.

There was a nearer radiant glow which he thought was Hawthorne. That faded quickly but one or two annoying blobs of light in the sky remained too long for comfort. He prayed fervently that there were no enemy planes on their way for a raid.

Below him near the parked cars a woman was arguing hysterically about her need to get home to her children.

"It's no use arguing, you can't go," a man's voice said firmly.

"I'm going," she cried insistently.

"In case you haven't heard, we're in a war. The army needs the roads at a time like this. They won't stop for you or get out of your way. They will go through. They have military things to think about. If you have any regard for your children, you won't run the risk now or any other time of getting hurt and perhaps killed."

The woman came running up the steps and dashed past Percy. He followed her inside. He heard Gloria talking to a man. Percy touched Gloria's arm and told her who he was.

"Hello, Percy," she said. "It's a nuisance, isn't it?"

"Rather. I was keeping my eye out for you. Will you need me now?"

"No. Everything seems to be all right."

"I didn't mean this, I meant later," he explained.

"Oh," she cried. "Oh!"

"I happened to overhear your promise to go away with Christopher."

"I'm not going with him," she stated firmly. "I very nearly made a fool of myself, but that is a thing of the past now. I'm *not* going. I feel free for the first time in months, free! He is out of my system. I can't explain it to you, but Christopher's power over me seems to have been cut away. I think you did cure me. I can see myself in an entirely new light now; I realize the things about my feelings for him which you tried to make me understand. It seems to be all in the past. Don't worry about me any more, I'm going to be all right and I'm not afraid of Christopher."

"You're really sure you won't go with him?" he asked.

"Positive. I did agree to go back to him. Not five minutes later I saw him kissing another woman. He sounded his death knell as far as I'm concerned."

"If it's any consolation to you, you are absolutely right. You would not have been happy with him," he assured her.

"I know it now. Thank you, Percy, for all you've done. If it had not been for you I would have been miserable again. Do you know I feel a little like a prostitute as I realize certain things about myself."

"That's hardly the word," he refuted stoutly.

"But that's how I feel. I want to get home and have a bath, mentally and physically, to feel clean again."

The crowd of jostling shapes had thinned out, moved away.

"Where is everyone?" she inquired.

"Hard to tell in this dark. Most have gone to the auditorium, I suppose," he replied.

"We had some difficulty getting our victims untied in the dark," she laughed. "I tried to tell them that it was good practice. Claude Stevens didn't think so. His team was caught by the janitor's office. He was trussed up and fuming to be loosened so that he could take up his work as an auxiliary policeman. We had a few granny knots." Amusement was rich in her voice.

"That knot on Christopher was especially good," he said.

"Was it?"

"Good Lord!" he exclaimed. "Didn't you untie Christopher?"

"No."

"We left him in the room upstairs."

"I know."

"Didn't the other team go up for him?"

"No. Your team was quicker than the others. We disbanded on this floor."

"Poor devil!" Percy exclaimed. "He's still up there."

"And a good thing for him if he is," she said. "He's probably enjoying himself."

"We should untie him. He won't be able to move. Both legs were splinted. Ruth tied his hands together in a particularly tight granny knot. I'll go up and free him."

"He has probably had at least six women from the sewing class hovering over him," she said. "Either he can take care of himself or get other women to do things for him." She went away in the darkness.

Regardless of his personal feelings about Christopher, Percy wanted to make sure that Christopher had been released. He started across the lobby for the stairs and collided with a woman. She asked him the location of the telephone. He guided her to the booth under the stairs.

He started back into the lobby but before he had reached the foot of the stairs a dark bulk came hurtling down and rolled over on the floor just in front of him. A woman screamed. People groped forward. Percy felt his way along the floor toward the dark object and knelt down. It was a man.

Behind him, like a moving wall, he felt the groping, curious people. "Keep back," he warned. "Someone has fallen down the stairs."

"I was tripped," a voice moaned from the floor.

A flashlight came on and played over the body. It was the principal of the school.

"Mr. Hewing!" several voices exclaimed in unison.

"Put out that light!" Billings' voice growled from across the lobby.

"But Mr. Hewing has been hurt," a woman protested.

"Can't help it. Put out the light. Do you want a bomb dropped on all of us?"

Nervous complaints filled the gloom, but the light went out. Gloria came through the darkness and knelt beside Percy.

"I think it's silly that we can't have a light." A thin high voice came floating down the staircase. "There are no bombs or anything."

Percy recognized the voice. It belonged to little Fanny Hayes, who seemed to be the living counterpart of the character Gracie Allen played on the radio. As a matter of fact, Percy thought of the girl as Gracie and often called her by that name.

"We'd better move him into the auditorium," Gloria suggested. "I'll get the emergency stretcher and some helpers."

In the brief moment of light Percy had seen blood down the front of Hewing's shirt. All the things he had learned in the First Aid class raced through his mind, particularly the admonitions: never move a victim until you have determined the extent of his injuries. Additional injuries are often caused by the zeal of people to help. Be particularly cautious after a fall.

"Get a doctor," he called into the darkness, "and hurry!"

He bent over Hewing's head and asked, "Is your nose bleeding?"

"No," Hewing replied. "There's a cut on my hand."

"Which hand is it?" he asked.

Hewing's left arm came up as he said, "The right one."

Percy asked casually, "Can you raise your right hand a little?"

"No," he replied. "I can't move it."

A broken arm as well as a cut, Percy diagnosed. He moved to the right side of the body and applied digital pressure.

"Here's the stretcher," Gloria announced out of the darkness. Her voice was calm. "How is he?"

"Fine. He has a cut on his right hand and I rather suspect a fracture of the same arm. Get help. I'll take care of the arm. We'd better get him into the auditorium where there is light."

They carried Hewing into the auditorium. He was covered with blood. He had a bad cut across the base of his fingers on his right palm. It had been bleeding severely. "I'd better apply a tourniquet," Percy said.

Mrs. Billings handed him a triangle bandage which he adjusted at once.

"Where are your blankets, Mrs. Billings?" he asked.

"Wouldn't you know I wouldn't have them when they were needed, after lugging them around like a St. Bernard for months," she said with disgust.

"Please get some," he said.

Gloria had been busy dressing the cut hand, talking to Hewing as she worked, smiling down at him.

"Keep him covered," she said looking up from her work, "and warm."

"I must get up and take care of things," Hewing protested. "I'm responsible for all these people."

"We'll take care of everything, you stay right here," she said firmly as she finished the bandage.

"But . . ." he began a new protest.

"It's useless to argue," she said with gentle authority. "You are in our hands and we won't let you get up until the doctor comes. You have a broken arm. You're going to stay right where you are and I'm going to stay with you to see that you do. If I have to leave you I'll place someone else on guard."

"Are you leaving with Christopher right after school?" he asked Gloria.

"School isn't over and I'm not leaving the job. I've changed my mind. I'm not going away. I'll take that new First Aid class next week, if you still want me here in the school."

"Not going away!" he said with surprise. "Not leaving! Of course, I want you, here in the school, but I thought . . ."

"I know what you thought."

"You said that you . . ."

"I've changed my mind. It's all right. Don't worry about me if you have already made arrangements to replace me."

"Arrangements," he repeated slowly. "There hasn't been time. I've done nothing. I'm glad you're staying." He smiled.

"I don't think you ought to talk so much," she cautioned.

"There's nothing the matter with me," he insisted as Percy released the tourniquet and watched the dressing on the hand to see if the bleeding had stopped.

"We're going to be positive that you are all right," Percy told him. "Your tumble down the stairs, your cut hand and your broken arm are enough for one night."

"How did it happen?" Gloria asked.

"Yes," Percy said. "You said that you had been tripped. Are you sure about that?"

"Definitely sure. Something was poked between my legs as I fumbled with my foot for the top step. I felt myself going and grabbed for the railing. My hand went through and beyond the banister rail and clamped down on the ornamental work. I gripped hard to keep myself from going but I had lost my balance. I guess my arm must have snagged between the rail and the ornamental iron work which cut me."

"Who on earth would trip a person in the dark that way?" Gloria asked indignantly.

"Some practical joker," Hewing suggested.

"Practical joker," she scoffed. "A person with that type of humor ought to be in jail."

Hewing had ceased to be a novelty to the people assembled in the auditorium. They were restless; moved about aimlessly.

"We ought to provide entertainment for them," Hewing suggested. "We must arrange a program in case this happens again. The time will pass more quickly and in the event of a raid it is better for people to have something to occupy their minds."

It would be difficult to imagine how the big, generous-minded principal could attract enmity, but Percy had to put the question,

"Have you any enemies in the school, Hewing? I can't accept your idea of a practical joker."

Hewing turned his head and regarded Percy with surprise.

"For goodness' sake, Percy, don't be so murder-minded," Gloria said rather sharply. "Because you've been involved in a couple of murder cases, you're inclined to think the simplest thing is a setup for murder."

"Hewing's fall was not a simple thing," Percy reminded her. "It was not a practical joke. I believe it was done on purpose. Hewing's fall might have killed him."

"I have no enemies, at least I'm aware of none," Hewing assured him.

"Did you see anyone when you were up there?" Percy asked.

"No. There were a number of people of course, but I

didn't recognize more than one or two voices. They were all somewhere near the head of the stairs."

"Did you see Christopher Smead?"

"No."

"Would you recognize his voice?"

"Why yes, I think I would," Hewing admitted.

"It can't be possible that he's still tied up," Percy said to Gloria.

"Who?" Hewing demanded.

"Christopher. We left him in room 244," Percy explained. "You saw him when we carried him up, remember? Well, he's still like that."

Hewing made an effort to rise but Gloria's hand restrained him. "But Smead must be released," Hewing insisted. "I can't have him forgotten."

"I'll go," Percy promised.

"Ten to one there's an angel with him," Gloria said lightly.

She's trying to prove to me that she's cured, Percy thought as he hurried up the aisle.

He paused for a moment when he left the auditorium to accustom himself to the darkness. He took a few short steps forward and was greeted by a little squeal.

"You bumped into Fanny," a voice giggled.

It was Fanny Hayes, again.

"It's all right, Gracie," he said absently.

"Oh, Mr. Peacock, you always call me Gracie. That's why I can tell who you are in the dark. Why can't you remember that my name is Fanny? Goodness knows we hear enough about fannies," she burbled.

Fanny gripped his arm. "Exciting, isn't it? Do you think we are being bombed?"

"I haven't heard any yet," he said, shaking himself free of her clasp.

"Did you see the planes that other night when the guns

were shooting?"

"No."

"I did. I counted twenty."

"That's remarkable, Fanny. Truly remarkable. I don't see how they existed in that barrage of shell fire, but if you saw them . . ."

"That's what my father says. He was looking into the sky at the same time. He says I'm always seeing things."

"He ought to know," Percy muttered.

"Nobody ever believes me. . . ." she sidled close to him, laid her hand on his sleeve and mewed confidingly. "That's why I wouldn't tell anybody but *you* about the ghost I saw." She had been walking beside him toward the lobby.

"What ghost? Do you mean the rider of the hills? Tell me where you saw it. I'd like to have a look."

"Oh, that one. I don't believe that hooey, do you?"

"Many people claim to have seen it," he reminded her.

"Well, I haven't. I've never looked for that one. I mean right here in the school. Upstairs. Just now. Well, a little while ago."

"What?"

"Yes. Just a little while after the lights went out. I was up there. I was looking for the stairs when I thought I heard voices, sort of low-like but I wasn't sure. I looked back down the hall."

"Do ghosts talk?" Percy interrupted.

"Now you're making fun of me. It was sort of white, the thing I saw. It flitted across the hall and it looked like a ghost to me. I was awful scared. I saw it go back across the hall again."

"A criss-cross ghost. You were very brave to wait for a second apparition."

"I wasn't brave at all. I couldn't move. After it disappeared the second time I heard a sort of squeal and then a low laugh and the ghost darted again."

"It seems to have been a very busy ghost. How did you see all that in the dark, or was there some light?"

"There wasn't any light. My father says I have cat's eyes on account of the way I can see in the dark."

"I'll say you have," a voice boomed at them.

It was Marjorie Blake and her voice, like her body, was large.

"Goodness! You frightened me!" Fanny squealed.

"I hope it's permanent," Marjorie bellowed disgustedly and marched toward the office.

"She sounds mad. I didn't do nothing to her," Fanny complained.

Marjorie was furious. They could hear her voice rolling through the lobby as she stood at the office and demanded, "Is Miss Kelton or any member of the sewing class here?"

There were low murmuring answers.

"Well, why in the name of heaven didn't someone remember that I was pasted up in that confounded paper form? Why did you all run off and leave me in such a predicament? A fine lot you are, all of you!" Her blast had a scorching quality; the words snapped and sparked. "Thanks to you, I've had an experience, I can tell you!"

There were soothing sounds, soft voices trying to make explanations but Marjorie paid no attention.

"Deliver me from any of you in a real emergency," she shot at them, "and the First Aid class is just as bad. Christopher Smead is still up there unless he's got his legs free from those splints. First Aid indeed!"

He saw her bulk move away from the office door.

"Are you sure Christopher is still up there, Marjorie?"

"You heard what I just said," she snapped. "It's all partly your fault for opening that door. You peeping Tom!"

Fanny giggled.

"It's no laughing matter, you young snippet."

"I don't know what it is, but snippet yourself!" Fanny retorted quickly.

"Marjorie," Percy cut in. He didn't want a female row on his hands. "Why didn't you release Christopher? You've done the same thing to him that these others did to you—left him flat."

"Ask *him* why I didn't release him?" she snorted. "He can rot for all I care. The impudent thing!" She swung away from them.

"She doesn't like Christopher, does she?" Fanny whispered.

"I don't think she does," he agreed dryly.

"I don't either. He's supposed to be . . . Well, my father says no girl is safe around Christopher, but Christopher never made a pass at me."

" 'Men seldom make passes at girls who . . .' " Percy began.

"Oh, Mr. Peacock. I don't wear glasses," she giggled. "For a psychologist you're not a bit observing."

"Perhaps you're right," he agreed. "I'm going up to find Christopher, if he's still there. I'll also see if I can locate that ghost of yours. You stay here."

"I want to go with you."

"No. I don't want you. Stay here and use your cat's eyes. If you see Christopher or if I'm gone too long come up and find me."

"Do you think he was playing ghost?" she asked.

"Playing, perhaps, but not ghost. It's out of his line."

Her quick giggle rippled after him as he mounted the stairs.

Odd that Christopher should have remained quiet for so long—odd, unless Gloria had been right when she so surprisingly jested about an angel's being with him. Curious thing for Gloria to say, not like her at all, rather out of character. Perhaps she had said it to show him that she was completely cured. Anyhow, it was more than likely that some woman would be, had been with Christopher. As he approached the vicinity of room 244 he paused and called softly, "Christopher, are you there?" He waited but there was no answer.

He was tempted to go back to the lobby and forget Christopher. Perhaps he didn't want to be released or disturbed. The complete silence, however, bothered Percy. There was no movement, no sound of any kind. He paused in the door. The glass of the windows glistened against the night sky.

The dark outline of the stretcher was on the floor where they had left it. "Christopher," he called.

Christopher did not answer. The bandages on the splints caught the gleam from the windows and glowed brightly in the darkness. "Don't play 'possum," he said as he advanced into the room.

Christopher did not answer.

Percy took his pencil flashlight, cupped it in his hand and turned the feeble ray toward Christopher. "Good Lord!" he cried.

Christopher could not answer. He was saturated with blood. His throat had been cut.

For a moment Percy was in a panic. Then he remembered the many oft-repeated things he had heard in First Aid classes. A sense of utter helplessness overcame him but that passed as he dropped to his knees and adjusted the tiny flashlight on the mound of the blanket which had been thrown over Christopher. He let his hands grope forward.

"I've got to stop the blood," he told himself as his fingers searched for the severed arteries. "This isn't sterile, my hands are full of germs," was his next thought. But he didn't stop. He found the main artery and clamped it between his thumb and finger.

He needed help. He knew his hand would grow tired, his fingers stiff. He filled his lungs with air so that he could make as loud a cry as possible. He was ready to shout when he was hit on the back of his head. His head seemed to whirl away from his body. He felt consciousness slipping away from him. "I can't," he fought. "I can't pass out. I must hold on." He tried to grip tighter on the artery but his fingers would not obey the impulse. They seemed far away, out of his reach. He remembered that a worker must not fall on his patient. There were so many things to remember; all of them raced through his mind as he sank deeper and deeper into the darkness.

III

SLOWLY HE SEEMED to be rising, to be taking shape and form. He heard a voice calling him from a long distance. It was very faint, as if someone were searching for him through a dark wood. He realized that he was listening hopefully. He waited for what seemed ages and then he heard it again a little louder. He tried to cry out, found himself struggling to make sounds but his throat muscles were constricted and would not function. That was it. A vague terror filled him. He didn't quite remember. His hand went to his throat, he shuddered. It was wet and slippery. He had a sense of being lost, abandoned. He was sliding back into the darkness again when the voice grew louder, became more than a sound. He heard words, definite words, silly words.

"I see you."

"Then why, oh why, don't you help me?" he asked mutely. He tried to speak but his lips wouldn't move.

"What are you doing?" More silly words.

"Dying," he thought, "dying and you ask me questions."

There was a giggle. Something in his brain clicked. "Gracie!" His lips moved. The sound of his voice startled him, roused him.

"Who is Gracie?"

"You are Gracie. Fanny is Gracie."

"Oh, Mr. Peacock!"

Quick anger mounted to confuse him. He shook his head to find that it seemed strange. It was large and was spinning. He felt his throat, clutched at his head to keep it from toppling off. Then he laughed hysterically. He remembered.

It was not his head that he must worry about. It was Christopher's head. He fought against weakness. He must do something but first he must control his resentment at Fanny's silliness. The dark place seemed ready for him again. He must not go back.

He fought hard to stay out of the darkness. He spoke slowly, measuring his words. "Fanny! Get help, quickly. Run! A doctor! Hurry! Hurry! Hurry!"

There were new sounds, hard-beating raps. He thought it was the pounding of his heart but realized, as the sounds grew fainter, that Fanny had made them as she ran down the hall. He lay still. He knew there was something he should do, something very important that should be done at once. If only his head didn't hurt so. If his eyes would clear and come out of the darkness. His thoughts were like knife edges cutting into his brain. He tried not to think but that hurt too. He counted ten slowly and carefully. His brain began to clear; he remembered.

He raised himself to his knees, felt about in the dark. He was beside the stretcher, beside Christopher. Christopher with his throat cut. Was it too late? How long had he been unconscious himself? He must do something for Christopher. Christopher was bathed in blood. Christopher was like the sunset tonight, all red, blood-red. Percy was dizzy as he leaned forward. He fumbled in the dark. His fingers revolted at the new touch of blood. He must make them obey his will. He heard excited voices, heard the scuffling of many uncertain feet in the dark, heard Fanny's sharp little voice saying, "This is the room."

He was never so glad to hear anything in his life.

In the surge of relief he realized what was happening, felt like a fool, was filled with shame but could not help it. He fainted.

When he regained consciousness he was flat on his back.

His feet were slightly elevated and he was wrapped in a blanket. Someone was sitting beside him waving a bottle of ammonia under his nostrils.

"I should say, 'Where am I?' " he thought, "only I know where I am. I'm in the school."

He lay quiet for a short time and then said to the person who continued to wave the bottle under his nose, "I'm all right."

"He's coming to," a voice said out of the darkness. It was Mrs. Billings.

"Oh! Goody!" That was Fanny.

"Thanks, Fanny," he said weakly.

"It wasn't anything. What did I do?"

"It was. . . ."

"You'd better be quiet," Mrs. Billings' low voice rolled over him soothingly.

"I'm all right." He tried to get up.

Mrs. Billings' two hundred pounds were behind the hand which pinned him to the blanket.

"You've had a crack on the head, you passed out and the doctor said to keep you quiet until he came back," she said. "I know it isn't in the text book but you're going to stay here if I have to sit on you to *keep* you down."

"Don't be a pancake," Fanny advised with a giggle.

"Don't you be flip," Mrs. Billings snapped.

"Christopher?" Percy asked.

"Don't know. The doctor didn't say. They carried him down to the auditorium."

"Fanny," he called. "Where are you?"

"I'm right here, Mr. Peacock."

"How long had I been gone before you came to look for me?"

"I don't know. It seemed like ages but maybe it wasn't, because things seem longer in the dark, don't they? Anyhow it was so quiet up here that I began to feel funny all over. I guess it was just a premonition because the more I thought about you and the ghost—well, the more . . ."

"What ghost?" Mrs. Billings demanded.

Fanny started to explain, but Percy broke in and answered Mrs. Billings' question briefly.

"Humph!" she snorted. "I never heard of a ghost cutting a man's throat or," she added, "banging another man over the head."

"Yes, that's right," Fanny agreed. "There's always something to be thankful for. I know I wouldn't want a bang on the head but if I were you, Mr. Peacock, I'd rather have a bang over the head than to have my throat cut by a ghost or anyone else. Don't you think so too?"

"Fanny. Can you talk sense?" Mrs. Billings demanded. "You've double-talked ever since you were a baby."

"Well, I would. That's what I mean," Fanny said. "Suppose . . ."

Percy interrupted the second rush of gush. "Fanny, will you go down, see the doctor, find out when I can get up? Tell him Mrs. Billings is sitting on me, that my ribs will probably be crushed. . . ."

"Oh, Mr. Peacock. She isn't sitting on you at all. You say the funniest things, doesn't he, Mrs. Billings?"

"Go along. He's only speaking figuratively," Mrs. Billings said with annoyance.

"Some figure!" Fanny flashed back, giggled and said, "All right."

"Don't tell anything to anyone," Percy warned. "Remember!"

"Okay." She skipped away.

"Sometimes I don't think she's as dumb as she pretends to be," Mrs. Billings muttered.

"Could she be?" he asked.

She chuckled. "That was a good crack about my figure."

"Fanny is Fanny," he said. "She is an astonishing girl."

Fanny's footsteps hollowed away.

Mrs. Billings sighed, seemed to settle down more comfortably. He heard her fumbling with her kit bag. "We don't need the ammonia any more," she said.

"What did they do with Christopher?" he asked.

"They had to take him to the auditorium—had to have light to see how seriously he was injured."

"But Billings wouldn't let us have even a flashlight downstairs after Hewing fell. How did they ever manage to carry him to the auditorium in this pitch-blackness?"

"Luckily, the first person Fanny bumped into was Dr. Klip at the bottom of the stairs. It's a mercy, isn't it, that he agreed to teach the elementary First Aid class, so that he was right here in the building when he was needed? Dr. Klip directed everything. I must say," she added, "that two members of your team, Alice Walker and that Higgins, were most efficient in helping out. In fact I must say that I was surprised at the way the advanced first-aiders took to the emergency.

"Not," she rambled on, "that Gloria isn't an excellent teacher, she is and we've all learned a lot, but somehow I didn't think it would work out this way. I didn't think most of them were interested in the work because up to tonight her class has been a disappointment to most of us."

"Has it?" Percy asked, surprised. "I thought it had been very successful."

Mrs. Billings' breath puffed over him in a short blast of exasperation. "Percy Peacock, don't lie there and pretend you don't know what I mean! You know perfectly well that a good ninety percent of us came to this advanced class because Gloria was the teacher and we heard that Christopher had enrolled for the course." He heard her hitch forward, grunt slightly. It was pleasant to lie there and let her words roll over him while he regained his strength and readjusted his thoughts.

"You know we've all had the standard course and have our cards," she said, "though how some of the women passed beats me. I wouldn't want to have Nancy Stevens put one of her bandages on me. No sir! And as far as artificial respiration is concerned . . ." She left her opinion unexpressed and went on with her first thought. "None of us needed the advanced course to be either a warden, a fire-watcher or an auxiliary policeman."

"I thought you all came because you wanted to know more."

"Phooey, to you!" She blew good-natured scorn at him. "You know that people are saying that we won't be bombed, that all of this is sheer nonsense, that most people don't want to think that anything can happen to us . . . the ostriches!" She snorted contemptuously. "I can't stand such an attitude. I'm all for being prepared even if it never happens, but we might as well look things squarely in the face and realize that a lot of people right here in this community feel that they are wasting their time in this work. I don't think we are but . . ."

"We aren't wasting time. We should prepare, no matter what we think," he insisted.

"Of course we should, but that has nothing to do with what I said about this class."

"You're interested in people?" he suggested.

"Of course I am. Gloria and Christopher may have been a psychological case to you but to most of us they were two people who had been wildly in love and had run headlong for a smashup. They were something to talk about while we fixed Bundles for Blue-jackets and did Red Cross bandages."

"You're honest about it."

. "Of course I am. Up to tonight nothing of interest happened. Christopher did not seem to rouse one spark of jealousy in Gloria by running around with Ruth Teale the way he did." She leaned a little nearer. "As a matter of fact I think Christopher was the one who was jealous. At least things came to a head and made up for lost time. There were three or four little flare-ups. I'm sure Christopher was jealous of Henry Graham."

"I don't see why." Percy protected Henry, satisfied to let her talk while he thought of the things which had happened before the attack on Christopher.

"Then you're not so keen a student of human nature as you're supposed to be. Henry Graham is, always has been and always will be crazy about Gloria. Not that I blame him one bit. She's a lovely girl, pretty too. Any sensible man would have realized her fine qualities and made a success of the marriage. Christopher wasn't sensible. He took Gloria away from Henry in the first place. No. I don't know that she ever was Henry's girl, although Henry has been mad about her for years. She just fell for Christopher. Henry, however, has been teacher's pet all through this class."

"Henry was probably a good student."

"That had nothing to do with it. I think she was nice to Henry to keep Hewing away from her. Hewing's been quite devoted, they tell me, though I haven't noticed it myself." She sighed heavily. "Gloria fooled all of us. We thought she'd go back to Christopher." She leaned as close to him as possible. "She did go out with him several times."

"Why not?" he asked.

"Are you just trying to irritate me or did that crack on your head do something to your common sense? She was risking her peace of mind by going out with him. He had something that appealed to women; that is, most women," she added quickly. "He never appealed to me. I've never felt comfortable with a handsome man, they always seem sort of uncontrollable, and no matter what I think of Christopher I must admit he was handsome. I can't understand why the movies didn't gobble him up."

"He was not photogenic," he said and realized that he, too, was speaking of Christopher in the past tense. "Women made Christopher what he was," he added.

"Of course they did," she agreed. "Fawning over him the way they did, believing his nonsense. It was enough to turn the head of any man. Why, I saw things in this class . . ."

What it was she had seen she did not bother to state as her mind went back to her original thought. "It sounds heartless to be talking this way about him. We expected fireworks, but I don't think anyone dreamed of murder."

"Why do you say murder? We don't know that he's dead. Klip—the first aiders—" his voice trailed off.

Mrs. Billings snorted derision at Percy's optimism.

"Well, his throat was cut, wasn't it? You were banged over the head. Ever hear of anyone living when his throat has been cut for him?"

"Christopher might have cut his own throat," he suggested.

"I'll have the doctor examine your head again," she said. "You know Christopher wouldn't ever commit suicide. I don't have to be a professor of psychology to know that. He liked himself too much to hurt himself. He was real vain."

Percy smiled at the rightness of her statement.

She sighed again. "I wouldn't want to be in Gloria's shoes—."

He was startled. He interrupted her quickly, "Why Gloria?"

"Well, why not? She was his ex-wife. She didn't change her name."

"The court has not granted the final decree," he reminded her.

"They didn't get along when they were married and living

together. She was jealous. Things have been going on."

"Gloria isn't the murdering type," he said.

She laughed. "Neither am I, but there are times when I could annihilate Billings."

"He didn't like Christopher, did he?" he asked.

"Who?"

"Billings."

"No." She seemed to say it guardedly as if she were thinking carefully. "Few men did," she added after a moment.

"What did Christopher do to Billings, flirt with you?"

"Don't be funny. I'm fat and fortyish." There was a long pause which she finally broke. "Why did you ask that about Billings?"

"I was wondering. Billings was upset at Christopher earlier in the evening. As a matter of fact he said he didn't see why someone didn't kill Christopher."

"Just talk," she said quickly. "People talk too much, say things they don't mean—just as I did a moment ago."

He sensed a new uneasiness in her manner. "She's disturbed because of Billings. She knows something about the two men and she's worried," he decided.

Fanny's quick giggle came floating down the hall, rippling over the quick pounding of her heels.

"Here comes Thin-Brain," Mrs. Billings said.

Percy tried to get up, but her arm shot out and he was gently pushed back to the stretcher.

He smiled as he heard her get to her knees, then grunt as she rose to make room for the doctor. After a brief examination Klip decided that Percy was fit enough to get up.

Percy sat on the side of the stretcher and asked, "What about Christopher?"

"Dead," Dr. Klip replied.

"I failed then," Percy regretted.

"No. I wouldn't say that. I think he was dead before you

found him—or rather you found him too late," Dr. Klip corrected. "I'm making—or rather I'm supposing that to be true—basing my opinion on the amount of blood he had lost."

"Have you notified the police?" Percy asked.

"The lines were all busy but I finally got a call through. Come down to the auditorium and I'll have a look at that head of yours."

Percy made slow work of getting to his feet.

"On second thought, we'd better carry you until I've checked," Dr. Klip decided.

"I'm all right," Percy insisted.

"One of the first things we learned was not to let a victim move about," Mrs. Billings reminded him. "Get down!"

He was glad to lie back without further argument.

"Does he need a blanket over him, Dr. Klip?" Mrs. Billings asked.

"It will do no harm," he replied.

The blanket went over Percy.

"We three can manage the stretcher as far as the head of the stairs," Klip announced. "We can get additional help from the lobby. Do you know how to carry a stretcher?"

"Yes," Fanny purred. "I've had First Aid."

"Humph!" said Mrs. Billings. "I'll take the head, doctor, and you the foot. You can balance the side, Fanny."

At the stairhead other stretcher-bearers came and Percy was carried to the auditorium. After the darkness in the room above the sudden glare of light was unbearable. The brightness made the pain in his head a torment. Percy quickly closed his eyes and submitted to the doctor's examination. After looking him over thoroughly Klip allowed Percy to get up.

Mrs. Billings had been busy rolling her blankets. She had them tucked under her arms. Her kit bag hung from her shoulder. "Well, I'm fixed up like a St. Bernard again," she said and waddled up the aisle.

A blanketed mass on the floor in front of the stage held Percy's eye for a moment.

"Are you going to solve the murder?" Fanny asked. "I think it's thrilling, don't you?"

"Please, Gracie," Percy said. "This is serious business."

"I'll say it is," she agreed. "A cut throat is serious any day." She looked at Percy. "It was serious enough to kill him, don't you remember? No, you don't. Well, as I said before, you were lucky. Say, I wonder why he didn't cut your throat too?"

"I've been wondering about that myself," Percy replied. He turned to Klip. "Where is Hewing?"

"We carried him to his office. He has had quite a shock. We splintered his arm. I told them to keep him quiet. I think I'll have a look at him now."

As they moved up the aisle, curious faces turned in their direction. Klip said, "As soon as the all-clear sounds I'll take Hewing in to the hospital and set the break. It's a wonder he didn't crack his neck."

"Tripping him was a foul trick," Percy said.

"Fair is foul, and foul is fair," Klip quoted. "Both you and Hewing were lucky that you weren't killed. I don't know much about the technique of murder but I'd say that you're still in danger. The murderer was taking no chances of discovery and he'll take none. What you need is a bodyguard, both of you. I'm glad I know nothing about it."

"You may be right and, if you are, Gracie is involved in the danger. What a dunce I was not to have thought of that myself."

"What are you talking about?" Klip demanded.

"You made me think of something." He turned and beckoned to Fanny who was looking after them. She came racing to them.

"Come with us," Percy said.

When they reached the lobby he led them to the center of the hall and bending close to Fanny whispered, "Go into the office and wait for me. I'll be there in a few minutes, and Gracie, don't talk. I know it's difficult for you to keep quiet, but don't tell anyone any of the things you told me."

"You mean about, you know, up, you know where?" she asked.

"Cat's eyes," he replied.

She giggled.

"No ghost, no squeal, no laugh," she answered.

"After all this mumbo-jumbo I'm not so sure your head's all right," Klip said anxiously.

"Gracie and I understand each other, don't we, Fanny?"

Klip was bewildered as she replied, "Oh, Mr. Peacock, tell me, who was Gracie, because you have her on your mind all the time?"

"Some other time," he promised. "Now, do as I say."

"Okay. No this, no that, no ghost, no cat," she said as she moved toward the office.

"Extraordinary!" Klip murmured as he followed her.

Percy went out onto the steps. There were a great many people sitting on the cold stone, discussing the murder. The cool night air felt refreshing. He leaned against the building and thought over what had happened, tried to put the pieces together to find some answer, if he could, to the riddle. Billings, Ruth, Henry, Gloria and Claude Stevens (who, Gloria had told him, had been fuming to be loosened from his knots so that he could take up his post as auxiliary policeman) were the first names which came to him. One of them might be the murderer. The police would want to talk to them, would want to ask questions.

He knew it would save time if all the people in the First Aid class were at the school when the police arrived but he had no authority to ask them to stay. He decided to check with Bill Dunning. He went back into the lobby in search of the telephone booth. His hand slid over the surface of the wall and into the dark hollow of the booth.

There was a frightened gasp, a gasp sodden with tears. "I'm sorry," he said. "I wanted to use the telephone."

"It's all right," a woman's voice said. "I'm through."

"Your voice is familiar," he said, "I'm Peacock."

"I thought you were," she said coolly. She slipped out of the booth. He put his hand up to help her but she avoided it, shrank away from him.

"It's Ruth, isn't it?" he asked.

"Yes, and I'm all right." She slipped away from him, hurried into the shield of the darkness.

He watched her go for a moment.

"Tears for Christopher," he thought as his coin rattled into the box.

IV

PERCY MADE THREE unsuccessful attempts to get the police. He gave up trying and groped his way back toward the principal's office.

"Hello!" Fanny greeted him as he came through the door. "I haven't said a word about you know what."

"Good. Is the doctor still here?"

"Yes." Klip's voice came through the darkness. "Anything wrong, Peacock?"

"No. How is Hewing?"

"I'm all right," Hewing's voice replied.

"We're taking him in to the hospital. I don't want to wait any longer and I don't dare set that arm here."

"I won't go until this blackout is over," Hewing protested. "The school is my responsibility."

"And you are mine. If you don't stop fussing about your job you'll worry yourself into a fever. Your arm must be fixed. We'll bring you back. Is that stretcher ready, Mrs. Smead?"

"It's right here," Gloria said.

Her voice seemed lifeless and dull.

"I don't need a stretcher, I can walk."

"We'll carry you, nevertheless," Klip stated bluntly. "You haven't shown much shock reaction yet but you will, so do as you're told. On the stretcher with you. You said there was a station wagon here which could be used as an ambulance, didn't you?" he asked Gloria.

"Yes, mine," she replied.

"Get it ready and send in people to carry the stretcher."

"I can help," Percy offered.

"No. We don't know how you're going to feel either," Klip said tersely. "You might collapse suddenly and then what would happen to Hewing? Bring in four people for the stretcher," he called after Gloria, who had moved toward the door.

"I'm getting sick of this darkness," Fanny whispered. "While I can see pretty well, it isn't like being in the light. Nothing is happening. Why do we have to sit in the dark?"

"The army will let you know some time, perhaps," Percy replied.

Hewing's stretcher was on the walk ready to go into the ambulance when the all-clear sounded. Within a minute headlights were snapped on and cars began racing away. In the spot of one set of lights Percy saw Mrs. Billings out in the middle of the road talking earnestly to her husband.

"You'd better come back here," Percy said to Gloria after she had superintended Hewing's entrance into the station wagon. "The police will want to talk to you."

"All right," she answered softly. Her hand rested on his arm a moment. "Will you have to tell them about us, Chris and me?"

"No."

"Will I?"

"I'm afraid so."

"Even what I said about his death knell?" she asked fearfully.

"That was not important."

"But wouldn't the police think it was if they knew? It has been haunting me ever since it happened." Her hand dug into his arm. "Percy, you don't think I killed him, do you?"

"No."

"Thank you." The relief in her voice was pathetic.

"Are you going to need any stretcher-bearers at the hospital?" Percy queried Klip.

"No. Are you ready, Mrs. Smead?"

"Yes."

"I'll follow you in my own car." He moved away.

"I'll come right back," she whispered to Percy. "I'll be back because I'll be terrified to stay away."

"There's nothing to fear," he assured her.

"Perhaps, but I'm horribly afraid just the same. Oh, Percy, help me!" For a moment he looked into her eyes. He tried to smile, to reassure her, but the torment in the blue eyes could not be dispelled by a smile. She was ridden by fear.

"Don't worry," he said. "Dunning is a friend of mine."

He watched the station wagon as it rolled away. "I'll have to be careful," he told himself. "Bill will snag right onto the notion of her as a suspect, will cling to the idea, will pursue it until I can show him that she did not cut Christopher's throat. But can I prove it?"

"Are you going to solve the murder?" Fanny asked at his elbow.

"I don't know, Fanny. I was wondering about it. We'll have to wait for the police."

"Why didn't you want me to talk?"

"Because you might be in danger."

"Why?"

"Don't tell anybody how well you can see in the dark."

"Everybody knows that. I've already told them."

"Gracie, how would you like to be a corpse?"

"Oh, Mr. Peacock, you say such funny things. I wouldn't know anything about it, would I, whether I liked it or not?"

"Fanny, stop your chatter!"

"Yes, sir."

"And listen to me."

"Okay."

"Mr. Hewing was tripped and might have been killed."

"And you were bashed over the head," she added.

"Exactly! The murderer is and will be desperate. If he thinks you know anything, then you might be next."

"People don't give me credit for knowing very much," she said simply.

"You should be thankful for that and let's hope the murderer is one of those people."

"What people?"

"The people who think you are a nitwit. Now, unless you want to be pushing daisies, don't say anything more about the ghost you think you saw, your ability to see in the dark or the cat's eyes. Don't remind people of those things."

"All right."

"Do you remember to whom you talked?"

"Just people, nearly everybody. It was dark. Remember? There was a lot of excitement when you were found, first because of you and then because of Christopher. They asked me questions and I told them. Goodness! How was I to know?"

"But you knew there had been a murder."

"Well, not exactly. Because his throat was cut, it didn't make it a murder, did it, until Dr. Klip found out that he was dead?"

"I suppose not," he agreed hopelessly. "Come along with me. Sit in the office until the police arrive. I'm going to look things over."

"Can't I come?"

"No."

They met Marjorie Blake. She had just come down the stairs and was barging across the lobby.

"Would you mind waiting a little while, Marjorie?" he asked.

"I certainly would. I don't want to see this school again or any of these people."

"I think the police will want to question you," he said.

"What for?"

"You were up there. You may have been the last person to see Christopher alive."

"If you call fumbling around in the dark seeing, I don't," she snapped.

"Then let's say you heard him alive. Of course, I have no authority to keep you here but if you stay it will make it much easier for the police."

"And I don't give a damn about the police. If I sit around here with this damp thing stuck to me I'll have pneumonia and then I won't be worth a tinker's damn to the police or anyone else."

"Are you still in the—er—dress form?" he asked.

"What's left of it and . . ." she sneezed. "There, that's the beginning of it. I'll probably be dead by morning. You know where I live." She turned and marched away.

"I've a good mind to go with her," Mrs. Billings said.

She still had her rolled blankets under her arms. She took a step toward the door then changed her mind.

"She looks like a blimp," Fanny whispered.

"Go back in there and behave yourself," he ordered.

He was waiting at the top of the steps when Bill Dunning came bounding up. Bill still looked like a life guard. He was tall and well molded, with friendly brown eyes which smiled at you out of his large, darkly tanned face.

"What do you know, Perce?" he asked.

"Not much."

"How does it look?"

"Bad. You don't see much in the dark, you know."

"It was a blackout murder, eh?"

"Definitely."

"When did you get here?"

"I was here all the time."

"You mean when the murder was being committed?"

"Yes."

"Gee, that's swell. We'll just wrap this one up and then go down for some coffee."

"Not tonight, we won't," Percy said soberly. "There are too many angles."

"Let's have them."

As they entered the lobby, Fanny advanced toward them. She smiled at Percy, then she became aware of Bill. Her eyes raced over his face, taking him in. She smiled again, at Bill this time. She looked at his jaunty cap and her eyes examined him down to his neatly encased legs.

"Is this the man who will want to ask me questions?" she asked eagerly.

"Presently," Percy said. "Go back to the office and wait for us. Can't you mind?"

She made a face at him. "All right," she agreed.

"I can't help being a schoolteacher at times," Percy said to Bill as he led him toward the stairs.

"Who is the cutie?" Bill asked.

"Fanny Hayes. She lives here in Palos Rojos, and I warn you, Bill, you're a marked man."

"What do you mean?"

"Fanny. She had that I-want-him look in her eyes when she saw you. She fell for you completely. Your number is up."

"You mean the little cutie? I didn't notice anything but a nice little kid. Just some of your ideas." Bill tossed the warning aside lightly.

"If I'm at the wedding, just remember that I told you so," Percy kidded with a grin.

"We won't worry about a wedding until we've settled

this business," Bill said. "Come on and tell me what you know about it."

After Bill's rapid examination of Christopher's body in the auditorium they moved upstairs. On their way up to room 244 Percy sketched for Bill what had taken place, and his own part in the tragedy.

"This is where it happened, eh?" Bill asked as they stepped into the room.

Percy nodded.

Bill had moved toward a few spots of blood on the floor. "What's that?" he asked, looking down.

"Probably my hand print," Percy replied. "I tried not to fall on him as I was losing consciousness."

"Too bad you got that sock on the head. Wonder what hit you?"

"Probably one of those," Percy suggested pointing toward the two-by-fours standing in the corner.

"Now, tell me this, Perce—as long as you were bashed over the head, why wasn't your throat cut too?"

"I've been wondering about that, Bill. I guess the murderer wanted to be sure that Christopher would die. If he put me temporarily out of commission he accomplished his purpose. If I had been in time I might have saved his life. But I have a feeling that I arrived too late to help Christopher. That's why I don't see clearly why I was hit. If Christopher had lived there would be no mystery."

"Why not? It was dark, wasn't it?"

"Yes, but I have an idea that the throat-cutting was an intimate job."

"You mean the murderer was well known to the victim, that the victim was not expecting to be ripped open, that he trusted the murderer."

"Something like that," Percy agreed. "Remember Christopher was bound hand and foot, completely immobilized.

Have you ever been splinted by a group of first-aiders?"

"No."

"When they immobilize they do a good job of it."

"Really hog-tied, eh?"

It was a grim jest if he meant it to be one.

"This probably belonged to the murderer," Bill pointed to Percy's pencil flashlight which had been crushed under someone's foot.

"That's mine."

"Too bad so many people had a chance to mill about in here," Bill regretted. "It raises hell with evidence."

Percy had been looking at the two-by-fours standing in the corner. They had not been planed smooth at the mill. One of them interested him. He was moving toward the sticks when the lights went out.

"What the hell!" Bill exclaimed. "Another alert."

They both listened. "No," Percy said. "It's probably a bad bulb."

"Bad bulb, hell!" Bill cried from the door. "All the lights are out and I don't like it. Come on!" He held his flash to guide Percy to the door and then started on a trot down the hall toward the main stairs and the lobby.

V

In the office Miss Conrad, Hewing's assistant, a flashlight in her hand, assured them that it was not another blackout.

"What's the matter with the lights?" Bill asked.

"I don't know. I've been trying to get the janitor, but he doesn't answer the telephone or the bell. I can't understand it."

"Where would he be?" Bill asked.

"In his room or anywhere in the building, closing up for the night, getting ready to leave."

"Where is his room?"

"Down the hall at the right. It's a small room just off the end staircase."

"Let's go," Bill said.

With the aid of his flash they were able to make good time. Bill started on a trot. Percy tried to keep pace with him until his head began to throb. He slowed down to a walk.

"What's the matter; getting old?" Bill called back.

A moment later Percy heard a shrill whistle and, forgetting his head, hurried forward. In the ray of Bill's flash he saw the janitor stretched out on the floor.

Bill dropped to his knees beside the man.

"Is he . . . dead?" Percy asked.

"No. Knocked out. He's been beaned, poor devil." Bill played the flash over the room until he located a switch board. "Throw that bottom switch, the one with the big handle, and see what happens," he suggested.

Percy followed instructions. The lights flashed on.

"Now, why was this done?" Bill demanded.

"The murderer wanted some extra time, in darkness," Percy hazarded. "Either in that room where we were or . . ."

"Or what?"

"Christopher!"

"What about Christopher? Why?"

"Perhaps there was something incriminating on Christopher, something the murderer had to have to be safe."

"Then we're too late now. If there was something in the auditorium we played right into his hands by leaving Christopher there without a guard. If it has to do with Christopher the murderer probably has it by now. In any event we can't leave this chap like this."

"Of course we can't. We've got to get a doctor."

"Right," Bill agreed. He reached for the telephone and gave his instructions. He looked at Percy and smiled. "This telephone connects with the office. That secretary dame is a flutter-pants. She insists there's an important call for me. Here it is."

He listened for a moment and replied, "Yes, this is Dunning." He listened attentively, nodded his head, said "yes" and "sure" at least a dozen times before he replaced the receiver with a groaning sigh.

Mrs. Billings and Alice Walker came. They had blankets. Mrs. Billings took out her ammonia and held it under the janitor's nose. "It's getting to be a habit," she said, smiling at Percy. "We can take care of him until the doctor comes."

As Bill and Percy went back along the hall Bill said, "You know, ladies with big backs shouldn't wear slacks."

"Perhaps they wouldn't if they were equipped with rear view mirrors," Percy replied.

As they neared the lobby Gloria hurried up to them. "I understand you have another victim," she said anxiously.

"How long have you been back?" Percy asked unexpectedly.

"Several minutes. Why?" she asked, obviously puzzled by his question.

"No particular reason," Percy replied.

Bill had stopped and was watching them. He too was considering Percy's question and her answer.

"This is Gloria Smead," Percy said. "The First Aid teacher."

"Oh, yes," Bill answered, "and related to the er—"

"Nearly an ex-wife," she said.

Gloria was uncomfortable under Bill's close survey. "Anything I can do?" she asked.

"Better attend to the janitor until the doctor comes," Percy suggested. "He's in his office. Billings and Walker are with him."

They continued on their way to the auditorium. "She's a very lovely looking woman," Bill said, as he passed through the black curtains into the auditorium.

"It was something on Christopher that the murderer wanted," Percy said as they went down the aisle. The blanket which had covered the body had been pulled off and thrown to one side. Christopher's wallet lay on the floor in a litter of papers and cards which it once contained.

"All this junk was shaken out of the wallet," Bill said. "What do you suppose the murderer wanted?"

"It wasn't money," Percy said. There were several large bills on the floor. He reached for the blanket.

"Don't touch it," Bill warned. "We'll want pictures of everything just as it is." He turned away. "Come on. We'll hang around the lobby until the boss gets here."

"Boss?" Percy asked.

"Yes, Trenton. Why did you ask Mrs. Smead when she came back?" Bill asked.

"No particular reason," Percy evaded.

"Your mind doesn't work like that, Perce. Do you think she did this?", His head jerked back toward the body on the floor.

"No. Lord no!"

"Then why did you ask?"

"I was afraid that *you* might think she did it," Percy answered honestly.

"What I think isn't going to make much difference."

"What do you mean, aren't you going to have the case?" Percy asked.

"No, I'm going to help Trenton. That was he on the telephone back there in the janitor's room. He wants to be in on this. He said to do nothing until he arrived."

"What's the angle?"

"Elections, I suppose," Bill replied. "Trenton is running again and he will want to keep himself before the public. There's nothing like a good murder for publicity. Trenton will know how to work all the angles." He stopped to listen to the shriek of a siren which came to a wailing moan in the plaza below. "That's the squad car now," he said. "His nibs will be along in a few minutes."

Bill met the men at the entrance, gave them their preliminary instructions, directed them to room 244 and the auditorium. Later he joined Percy at the entrance. "Let's have a smoke," he suggested as they moved down the steps.

"I'm sorry Trenton is coming in on this," Percy said.

"Why?"

"Many reasons."

"You're not worried about me, are you?" Bill asked with a grin.

"No."

"That's good because I'm used to it. I suppose I'd do the same thing if I were in his place."

"I doubt it," Percy replied quickly.

"Come clean, Perce," Bill said. "Whom do you want to protect?"

"Gloria."

"Why?"

"A lot of reasons."

"Do you suspect her?"

"No."

"Are you afraid of Trenton?" Bill asked.

"Yes, in connection with Gloria. I was even afraid of you. Will you try to keep your mind open?"

"Sure," he promised. "She doesn't look like a murderer."

"But she'll make excellent publicity material," Percy regretted.

"I suppose she will. This case is a mess, isn't it?" He glanced at Percy. "So are you. You're all smeared with Smead's blood. It's a good thing I know you or I'd run you in as suspect number one." His voice was gruff but his eyes were twinkling.

"Do you have any idea that I killed him?" Percy demanded.

"For the love of Pete, Perce. I know you. You're not the killer type."

"But I'm covered with blood, you just said. . . ."

"Forget it, can't you? I was just kidding." His eyes gleamed for a moment. "You couldn't very well hit yourself over the head that hard, either."

"Let's not get away from the point I want to make," Percy insisted. "You're willing to make mental concessions because you know me. I want you to do the same thing for Gloria, will you?"

"I might if you told me what you know about her."

"The things I know about her and Christopher are personal," Percy said, "but they are the things which, when brought to light by a clever newspaperman or an ambitious investigator, can be made to look very bad."

"Tell me about them," Bill suggested. "Advance knowledge is a good thing sometimes."

Percy gave him a quick summary of the married life of Gloria and Christopher.

"So she was afraid of him," Bill said after Percy had told him of Gloria's telephone call earlier that evening.

"No. She was afraid of herself. She recognized her weakness, a thing very few of us do."

"How could she be so crazy about him when he pulled his stuff right under her nose?"

"That, my friend, is a difficult question."

"I don't get it. Never did. He didn't like being married to her, for if he did he would have acted differently. She didn't like it or she wouldn't have walked out on him. They made a mess of marriage between them and yet tonight they were about to try it again. Why?"

"Perhaps it's a question of vanity. It must be very personal. He was a man well liked by women, yet he couldn't hold his wife. Men like her and yet she couldn't satisfy him. A man might try to make a mousetrap and give it up as a bad job, going on to something else, forgetting his first venture. We do that, but there are very few of us who are willing to admit our failures in dealing with people. We seem to think we can mold and influence other people, bend them to our way of life."

"But why should we be like that, that's what I want to know?" Bill insisted.

"Why are some people drunkards and others dope fiends?"

"You're telling me things," Bill reminded him. "I'm just asking."

"I only know certain truths about man. The rest is a riddle. I can't answer for, or explain, either Gloria or Christopher or why this had to happen. I've given you a sketch of their background and the things that happened tonight after I arrived here," Percy said.

"But you've explored all the possibilities of the relationship. You have been thinking about both of them. You know it was she who selected him as the victim and had him tied up. She knew where he was, she knew of his helpless condition. Am I right?"

"Yes."

"What a setup."

"True, it was a setup, but always remember that no one knew that there was to be a blackout tonight."

"Meaning what?"

"Isn't it rather obvious that the murder could not have been planned too far in advance?" Percy asked.

"I suppose so," Bill admitted. "Just how far in advance do you think?" he asked pointedly.

"That's something I don't know. I'd say this was a crime of almost immediate impulse."

"Just how long does an immediate impulse last? What does it mean?" Bill queried.

"Let's not be too technical. Let's call it a crime of passion. A crime committed while resentment and anger were still burning at a high pitch. With some people resentment burns itself out quickly, with others it may last indefinitely, smoldering sometimes for years until it is suddenly fanned into a flame."

"I begin to see why you're worried about Gloria," Bill said. "She fits into so many psychological angles of the case."

"Exactly," Percy agreed.

"So you want us to find other angles, other reasons, other impulses."

"Yes."

"So we'll have to start the old question-and-answer game,

begin to dig until we hit pay dirt," Bill mused.

"Beginning with what happened here tonight and going back," Percy outlined.

"And each step backward will tell us something more about Christopher and Gloria, will make us more suspicious of her," Bill reminded him.

"Which is my reason for urging upon you the importance of keeping an open mind."

They both listened. There was the imperious shrilling of a siren, harsh, constant. "That," said Bill, "is Trenton. He'll be here in a few minutes. It's his bloodhound voice hot on the trail."

VI

A SECOND CAR swung into the plaza behind Trenton's and ground to a stop. "The doctor and Hewing are back from the hospital," Percy announced as he saw them getting out of the second car.

"Now we can get going," Bill said with relief.

They climbed the steps beside Trenton. Bill briefly outlined the details of the murder, the second going-out of the lights, and the attack on the janitor.

"I'll have a look at the janitor," Dr. Klip said as they entered the lobby.

"And I'll get my work cleaned up," Hewing announced, turning into his office. How like Hewing, Percy thought with admiration, to get back to his job after the shock of that fall and injury! His dogged attention to duty was certainly remarkable.

Trenton was all breeze and bustle as he paused in the lobby and looked about. "Where do we begin? What have you done?" he asked Bill as his eyes measured Percy.

Bill introduced them quickly.

"Oh, yes, Peacock. I've heard about you. A theorist or something, aren't you—with an interest in murder?" Before Percy could reply to this sneer he went on, "Well, everything goes in a murder. What have you done, Bill?"

"Nothing," Bill replied. "I've been waiting for you to take over. The men are upstairs, doing the routine work. We ought to have their reports any time now."

"Ummm," Trenton mumbled. "I thought you'd have the case settled by this time. Well, we won't get done unless we make a start, will we? I want to know what happened. Who knows?"

"Peacock and Hewing," Bill said, "and the victim's ex-wife who was the instructor of the First Aid class."

"Are all the people involved still here?" Trenton demanded briskly.

"A few of them, but no effort was made to hold anyone," Bill informed him.

"Why not?" Trenton growled.

"The police weren't here," Bill replied.

Trenton swung toward Percy. "Since you're so familiar with murder cases, why didn't you keep the people here?" he demanded.

"I couldn't very well do that," Percy replied. "After all, I had no authority to do so."

"Someone should have done it. What was the matter with the school principal? He should have known."

"He was very much of a casualty himself," Percy remarked dryly.

"Well, then we'll start with him," Trenton announced and started for the office door.

Fanny stood just outside the door. She smiled with inviting coquetry at Bill as he approached. Her eyes were filled with a small child's hero-worship.

"Who are you?" Trenton demanded of Fanny. "And what are you doing here?"

"I'm Fanny Hayes. I've been helping Mr. Peacock with the murder." She replied in words so slurred by breathlessness that the whole sounded like one word.

"What do you know about the murder?" Trenton demanded.

"Well, I don't know anything about the murder but . . ."

"Come inside," he ordered.

In the office Hewing, looking strained and drawn, was checking school reports with Miss Conrad. Miss Conrad was probably forty, erect, rather sparsely built but pretty in spite of her tenseness. She had lovely grey-streaked hair which she wore in a fluffy pile about her head. She was efficient and considerate as she aided Hewing with the work he was doing. She held papers for him to sign, made things as easy as possible for him, favoring his injured arm.

Gloria was sitting in a chair just outside the rail which enclosed the inner office. Her hands were lying idly in her lap, her eyes fixed on a point over the heads of Hewing and Miss Conrad. Henry Graham was sitting beside her. His thin dark face was drawn, he was holding himself taut as if he were keyed for an ordeal which he knew he must face. He was watching Gloria. They turned as the group entered. For a fleeting moment her eyes caught Henry's and held them while she smiled at him reassuringly.

Hewing looked up from his work and slid his chair back a little from his desk. His arm hung in a sling from his shoulder. The white bandages made sharp contrast to the dark smears of blood on his blue shirt front.

"How are you feeling?" Bill asked cheerfully.

"Fine, now," Hewing replied, but the whiteness of his face belied his words.

"Can you tell us any of the things which led up to the murder?" Trenton asked bluntly.

"No," Hewing stated flatly.

Trenton gave Bill an accusing look. "Can anyone?" he asked impatiently, his eyes sweeping the room. "Well." His foot tapped the floor, accenting his impatience.

It was Fanny who spoke. She started in a vague preamble but stopped when she realized that Percy was scowling at her. The damage, however, had been done.

"Go on," Trenton ordered.

"I don't—know—what leads up to a murder," she stammered lamely.

"But you had something on your mind. What was it?" Trenton insisted.

"Well, in books—" she began.

"Never mind books," he growled.

"Anyhow it's the little things which count," she said, gathering courage, "and I guess I saw and heard a lot of little things tonight but I didn't know they were murder things when they were happening. You wouldn't know about a murder until after the murder had happened, would you? No, of course, you wouldn't and so . . ."

"What are you talking about?" Trenton growled.

"The murder," she replied, surprised. "It does sound silly, doesn't it?"

"I'll be the judge of that. Go on."

"Goodness! How can I tell you things when you stand scowling at me? You don't have to look like that, do you? Or is it something wrong with your face that you can't help?"

"There's nothing the matter with my face and I won't scowl. Now if you know anything about the murder, why don't you tell us so we can get on with the case?"

"Well, that's what I keep trying to do but you keep interrupting me all the time. This is all new to me and . . ."

Trenton groaned.

"See, that's what I mean. There you go again—one interruption after another. Now, it may not be important, but then who knows what is important in a case like this when so much happened and it was dark and all, but . . ."

She stopped to catch her breath, seemed to be rearranging her thoughts—if she had any. She smiled at Trenton as if she had forgiven him for the interruptions. He nodded back but his smile was sour. Behind his thin smile there seemed to lurk a desire to choke her to death.

"It started when I was on my way to school, the things which led up to the murder," she explained. "I was driving slowly because of the 'Save-Your-Rubber' campaign. You hear so much about it and see it in the papers all the time. That's why I noticed Christopher. He's the one who was murdered," she explained to Trenton. "He raced past me going about sixty, at least sixty, I'll bet, and that's no way to save tires. Right after he passed me I had to put on my brakes because I expected him to stop and if he had stopped we might have had an accident, if I hadn't put on my brakes, but he didn't stop."

"Why did you expect him to stop?" Trenton asked with remarkable control.

"Because of Ruth Teale," she said. "She was standing at the side of the road waiting for him."

"Why should he stop for Ruth Teale?"

"You wouldn't know that, would you? Because he has been bringing her to school every night ever since this class started and he's been taking her home, too," she added. "Everyone knows about that."

"Maybe they do, but I don't," Trenton growled.

"That's why I'm telling you, so you will know." She smiled brightly at him. "When he didn't stop for Ruth, I did. She was awful mad when she climbed into my car. Of course, I didn't say anything about him to her because I didn't want to hurt her feelings. Things were all right until we reached the parking place in front. Mrs. Billings, she's the fat lady who's down the hall with the janitor—you'll see her later— was coming toward us. She was out of breath; she walks to school," she explained.

"Get on with your story," Trenton prodded impatiently.

"Maybe Mrs. Billings wouldn't have waited for us if she

wasn't out of breath and, if she hadn't waited for us, then she wouldn't have said what she did."

Percy smiled as he saw Trenton's temperature rising.

"What did Mrs. Billings say?" Trenton asked.

"Oh, yes. I forget where I am when you keep interrupting me. Well, Mrs. Billings was surprised when she saw Ruth with me and she said, 'Why, Ruth, what are you doing with Fanny?' and Ruth said, 'If you must know, my boy friend passed me up.' She turned and ran up the steps, Ruth ran up, not Mrs. Billings."

"And do you think that has any bearing on the murder?" Trenton asked contemptuously.

"You don't know much about women, do you?" Fanny countered. "You don't know how mad Ruth was at him to say that. Anyhow, I'm not saying that Ruth killed him, I'm trying to tell you the little things because nobody else seems to know any of the things which happened."

"All right, all right! Get on! Only try to stick to important details," he advised.

"The next thing was the fight," Fanny announced and smiled appreciation as Trenton jerked alert and leaned forward with new interest. "Well, it wasn't really a fight, but it could have been a fight." Trenton's new interest evaporated in a long exhausted sigh.

"It was in the classroom; you know the advanced First Aid class. We were going to have an examination and I went up to the room early and there was Christopher; he's the one who was killed. I told you that, didn't I? Anyhow he was arguing with Henry. That's Henry over there." She pointed to Henry, who made an effort to look unconcerned.

Fanny smiled at Henry, unconscious of what she might be doing to him. "Henry and Christopher must have been having an argument because Henry said, 'Why don't you leave her alone?' He meant Gloria, Mrs. Smead, the teacher. Christopher said, 'Why don't you mind your own business?' He moved toward Henry and Henry gave him a push and Christopher sort of stumbled backward and knocked into a pile of splints which were on the front seat. Well, the splints fell to the floor with the worst bang and clatter you ever heard and Christopher grabbed one and swung at Henry. Henry saw it coming—didn't you, Henry?—and put his arm up so the thing didn't crash down on his head, but it did hit him and that's when the fight might have started, only Mr. Hewing came in just then and sort of walked between the two men and there was no fight. Mr. Hewing acted as if he hadn't seen what was happening, but he did, only he pretended and he said to Gloria, 'There's to be a faculty meeting right after school tonight.'

"I don't know why that made Christopher mad, but he turned on Mr. Hewing and said in a nasty way, 'You're doing that on purpose, Hewing.' He said it like that. Mr. Hewing was surprised, so Christopher said, 'Don't give me that innocent look. Do you think I'm a fool?'

"Mr. Hewing sort of just looked at Christopher for a minute and then said, 'I haven't quite made up my mind, Smead, but I think you are and always will be.' Henry laughed at that, which didn't make Christopher feel any better. Christopher followed Mr. Hewing out of the room.

"Mrs. Smead was upset, naturally, and she said to Henry, 'Don't let him row with Mr. Hewing, please.' So Henry followed them both."

"Was there a row?" Trenton asked Hewing.

"No, nothing more than has just been reported," Hewing put in promptly.

"There was another fracas," Fanny chirped. "Christopher got his face slapped."

"By whom?" Trenton demanded.

"Claude Stevens," she replied. "That was because Christopher was trying to bite Nancy's ear. Nancy is Claude's wife and Claude didn't seem to like it, although I wouldn't be too sure about how Nancy felt because she was giggling."

"Because Claude slapped his face?" Trenton asked.

"Oh, no, because Christopher was trying to bite her ear. As you know, if you've ever had anyone come up behind you and try to bite your ear, it tickles," she explained brightly.

"Fanny's tickling Trenton, I *don't* think," Bill remarked under cover of Trenton's grunt.

"None of what you tell me is exactly the cause for murder," Trenton said.

"I didn't say it was," Fanny retorted quickly. "I said it was the little things which led up to the murder. Of course, if you know why he was murdered there isn't any sense in my telling you about the . . ." She stopped and looked toward Percy.

"About what?" Trenton demanded.

"Should I tell him about—you know?" she asked Percy intimately.

Percy nodded. "You might as well tell him everything, Gracie," he gave up.

"There you go again," she laughed. "My name's Fanny," she explained to Trenton, "but sometimes he calls me Gracie."

"I can understand that," Trenton replied.

They all laughed except Fanny, who looked bewildered.

"Go on. You were going to tell us about the—you know —" Trenton prompted her.

"Well, Mr. Peacock and I have a secret." Trenton looked at Percy. "Well no," she corrected. "It isn't a secret because I told a lot of people and that wouldn't be a secret, would it? He told me not to talk about it."

"About what?" Trenton bellowed.

"I'm coming to it. If you're going to act that way I might

just as well go home. Of course, if you don't want me to help you . . ."

"Go ahead, only don't beat around the bush so," he complained.

"I'm glad you said that or I would have forgotten," she smiled at him. "It's a good thing you said 'bush' or I would have forgotten all about what I saw down in the courtyard."

Percy frowned. Fanny babbled on, "You don't know this, Mr. Peacock. I didn't tell you. I saw Christopher and Mrs. Smead in the courtyard talking. Naturally I was interested, we've all been interested in them on account of their split-up and all. I was on the second floor so I couldn't hear what they were saying but"—she addressed Gloria—"I saw him kiss you."

Gloria's face flushed rapidly. Percy caught Henry's quick glance of surprised anger.

"What if you did?" Trenton demanded.

"Nothing, then. I just saw it and then a little later, maybe five minutes . . ." She paused to consider the length of time and then decided that she had been right. "Yes, about five minutes later I saw him kissing Ruth Teale. You saw him too, didn't you?" she asked Gloria. "You must have seen them because I saw you stop in front of the door and look into the room."

"Yes, I saw it," Gloria murmured.

"I think I know now who the ghost was," Fanny burst out to Percy.

Everyone perked up at that remark.

"Don't tell me there's a ghost in this too," Trenton grumbled.

"No, not a real one. I think it was Marjorie Blake. She was having her form made. You know, one of those dummies they put dresses on. Well, I think she is the person I saw moving back and forth across the hall during the darkness."

"And what has that to do with the murder?"

"If it wasn't Marjorie, then maybe it was Christopher's spirit," she suggested, "because whoever it was, was coming out of the room where Christopher was, only I didn't know it then. I didn't know about the murder at all until after Mr. Peacock was hit over the head and I found him and then we found Christopher and he was dead."

"Where is this Blake woman?" Trenton demanded with a questioning look in Bill's direction.

"She went home," Fanny said. "Mr. Peacock told her she ought to stay but she said she didn't care about the police, that she was getting pneumonia from the form and she did sneeze and she said she might be dead by morning, didn't she?" She referred to Percy.

He nodded assent.

"You were around, weren't you?" Trenton said.

"Oh, yes. I was in the second-floor corridor when Mr. Hewing fell and all," Fanny replied brightly.

"It's too bad you didn't see something that mattered," Trenton commented viciously.

"I . . ." Fanny stopped. Her eyes went to Percy's, asked him a question, caught the negative movement of his eyes.

"Well, what were you going to say?" Trenton demanded.

She smiled slyly. "Nothing. I'm sorry if I didn't see anything important but then I wouldn't know what was important, would I, because this is my first murder and I don't know anything about murders, do I?"

VII

Trenton dismissed Fanny coldly and turned toward the door where Dr. Klip, the janitor, Mrs. Billings and Alice Walker were standing expectantly.

Percy was watching Fanny, wondering what it was that made her pause before she told something which would have been really important. She was talkative; she was a nuisance in many ways; but she had always been bright and alive. The little dancing lights had gone out of her eyes; she seemed smaller somehow as she slid back into her chair and looked cautiously about the room with speculative fear. He knew that something had occurred to her, some thought had swept all the nonsense out of her mind when she had started to speak and paused, looking to him for advice. He felt that, for the first time this evening, she had deliberately lied, had lied because of some personal fear. All her ramblings up to now had been impersonal as far as she, herself, had been concerned. She was playing the role of prima donna and had been enjoying the interest focused upon her, but the murder had never been real to Fanny, any of it, up until that moment of doubt.

"This man will be able to answer questions for you now," Klip announced to Trenton, indicating the janitor.

The janitor was short, dark and wiry. His skin was smooth, his eyes dark and round. A Mexican probably, Percy thought.

"What do you know about all this?" Trenton asked.

"Nothing. I was in my room when something hit me over the head," the janitor stated briefly.

"And you don't know who hit you?" Trenton queried.

"No."

"Where were you during the blackout?"

"In my office waiting for the signal to turn on the lights when the all-clear sounded."

"Did you go to the second floor at any time during the blackout?"

"No."

"Did you see anyone else go to the second floor during that time?"

He hesitated. "Some people went up the stairs just beyond my office. It was dark. I did not know who they were."

Trenton grunted his annoyance. "Do you know anything which might throw light on the murder and the attack on you?"

"No."

"You say some people went up the stairs during the blackout." He nodded. "Where did they come from?"

"They were people from the First Aid class. They had a man tied up."

Trenton's face brightened. "Was it the murdered man?"

"No. These people stopped just outside my office and deposited the stretcher when the lights went out. The man kept complaining because he wanted to be freed. He said he was a warden and had to be on duty. There was excitement and laughter among the others. They had trouble with the knots. To them it was a huge joke. I told them to carry him to the auditorium—that there were lights on in there."

"Did they take him?" Bill asked.

"No."

"Could you name anyone in that group?" Trenton asked.

"Only the teacher of the class," he replied.

"Why did you recognize her?"

"Because she asked me about the lights in the auditorium.

I explained that they were on a separate switch, that we had
had a new wiring job done because of blackouts."

"Then any of the people who were in that group knew
that the auditorium lights were not effected by throwing the
master switch," Trenton said.

"That's right."

"You did not recognize any of the others?" he asked.

"No, but the lady probably did," the janitor suggested with
a glance toward Gloria.

Trenton grunted. "We won't need you any longer, if you
have work to do."

"Will you be here long?" the janitor asked.

"We'll leave someone here all night but you need not
worry about that. Check with me before you leave the building."

As the janitor left them, Trenton turned to Gloria. "Now,
Mrs. Smead, suppose you tell us about that group outside
the janitor's room."

Gloria gave him the names of the members of that team.

"Who was the victim, the man who was tied?" he asked.

"Claude Stevens."

"I believe I have heard something about him."

"Yes, he's the one who slapped Christopher, I told you,"
Fanny cut in.

Trenton ignored her. "What did Stevens do when he was
released?"

"He left us at once. I think he went out through the door
at the end of the building, but I would not be sure," she replied.

"What did you and the rest of your group do?"

"We gathered our material, removed the stretcher so that
it would not be a hazard in the dark hall, and I suppose con-
verged toward the main entrance."

"What did you do?"

"I have just told you," she said evenly.

"The janitor states that some people went upstairs. Did *you* go upstairs?"

She hesitated for a fraction of a second before she said, "Yes, I did."

"Shy?" He popped the question at her explosively.

"I had responsibilities. My class was scattered about the building. I had equipment to worry about; I was doing my duty."

"Just what did you do on the second floor?"

"I went to my classroom, room 212. There was no one there. I·then came down to the lobby."

"You knew your ex-husband was in a room up there, didn't you? Why didn't you do something about trying to release him as part of your duty?" There was cunning calculation behind the question.

"I did not know that he was there at that time. He was taken up from the cafeteria by his team. Shortly after that the lights went out. It was later, much later, that I realized that he was still in room 244." Her eyes sought Percy's.

"As a teacher, as part of your duty." He emphasized the word "duty" meanly. "Did you go to him?"

"No. Mr. Peacock went up."

"Since you have stressed your responsibilities and duties, why didn't you go yourself?" he demanded.

He doesn't like her, Percy thought. He has fastened his suspicions on her already.

"She was giving me first aid," Hewing said gruffly. "I wanted to go, but she insisted that I keep quiet."

"She was right. Hewing had a broken arm and had had a bad fall. As a matter of fact he should not be here now," Klip announced. "He is due for a shock reaction."

Hewing suddenly became the center of interest.

"Tell us about that fall of yours, Fred," Bill suggested.

"I was at the top of the stairs, feeling for the first step—the next minute I was at the bottom," he said.

"You stumbled?" Trenton asked.

"No, I was tripped."

"I don't get it," Bill said. "Even though you were made a fall guy I can't understand your broken arm. You're one of the best tumblers I know."

Hewing smiled. "I was trying to protect my hand."

"If Mr. Hewing had known less about tumbling, he might have been killed," Klip said.

"How long after the alarm did you tumble?" Trenton asked.

"I couldn't say in point of time," Hewing replied after considering the question. "I ran upstairs to spread the alarm first and did several things after that."

"Don't you have a bell system—aren't you organized for just such an emergency?" Trenton demanded.

"The bell system was not working," Miss Conrad interrupted with an accusing glance in Hewing's direction.

"Why not? Had you been having trouble with the system?"

"No. We had had no trouble," Miss Conrad said sharply before Hewing could reply.

Bill walked through the gate in the office rail and walked to the board. He stood looking at it for a moment. "In case of an alarm, is it necessary to press all these buttons?" he asked.

"No." It was Hewing who answered. "There is a major control switch which is used in cases of emergency—fire-drills, that sort of thing. It is that switch at the bottom. By throwing that all the bells ring throughout the school."

"This one?" Bill asked and threw the switch.

Immediately bells began ringing and jangling sharply. The deep-toned sound of the gongs in the halls drowned out the more silvery peals of the smaller bells.

Hewing rose and walked across the room to the board. "That's strange!" He turned to Miss Conrad. "Has anyone tampered with the board?"

"If they did, I didn't see them," she replied crisply. "You forget that we were in darkness for nearly an hour and this office was filled with people, complaining, milling about, wanting to use the telephone."

Bill had released the major switch and turned to Hewing. The janitor came running to the door, excited, wondering what the sudden alarm might mean.

"Funny!" Bill commented after the janitor had been sent away. "Are you sure the bells wouldn't operate?"

"Positive." Hewing stated emphatically. "Miss Conrad received the call from the police station warning us that we were on the 'blue.' We had decided to dismiss the classes to give the people a chance to get to their homes but before we could do anything we were notified that we were on the 'red.' I ran to the board to sound the warning. I threw the major switch for the general alarm but nothing happened. I told Miss Conrad to find the janitor or throw the light switch herself and ran out to warn the classes. There was a First Aid group here in the lower lobby. I sent them out to warn the people in classrooms and ran to the second floor where I met Peacock and his group."

Bill had been tinkering with the board while Hewing talked. He opened a small door at the base of the panel and threw a switch. When Hewing had finished, Bill again pressed the major switch but no bells rang. He turned to Hewing, "Someone threw this cut-off switch."

Percy was very conscious of the look which Miss Conrad directed at Hewing. Her eyes seemed to say, "What are you going to do about it now?"

Trenton too must have noticed it, for he asked, "How about it, Hewing?"

Gloria rose and moved toward the gate into the closed section of the office.

Hewing scowled at her. Miss Conrad watched her with interest. Hewing put up his hand warningly, but Gloria paid no attention, "Mr. Trenton," she said. "They are trying to protect me. I asked Mr. Hewing—"

"Please," Hewing begged Gloria.

"It's no use. They must know," she cried. "They will find it out. It was foolish of me to ask you." She turned to Trenton. "I was giving my class an examination tonight. I asked Mr. Hewing if we could dispense with the bells."

"Why?"

"In order to carry out my plans I could not fit my time to the regular hours. We were to finish the first part of our examination and have our break before the scheduled time for recess. It was my fault that the bells did not ring. It had nothing to do with the murder."

"Why didn't you tell us all this in the first place?" Trenton growled at Hewing. "It would have saved a lot of time."

"That is also my fault," Gloria declared, holding Trenton's pin-pointed eyes with her candid blue ones. "On our way to the hospital to have Mr. Hewing's arm set we discussed the murder. We realized that the bells had aided the murderer, that we had aided unwittingly. Because of things which happened tonight, facts which Miss Hayes has given you, I saw the possibility of suspicion being pointed toward me. It seemed unnecessary to mention something which could have no direct bearing on the case."

"Don't you know, both of you, that it is bad business to block or obstruct the police?" he asked sternly.

Gloria flushed. "We had no intention of blocking you. We could not know that you would even think of the bells."

"It's my job to think of everything," he growled.

"Look, Fred." Bill directed attention back to Hewing.

"Since you knew about the switch having been thrown, why didn't you just readjust it and let the bells do the work for you?"

"It sounds silly now, but in the excitement of the alarm I forgot all about the switch. I suppose I was in a momentary panic. I know of no other way to explain it. I guess I had raid scare," Hewing admitted honestly.

"Of course you did," Miss Conrad agreed. "I know I did. I didn't remember about that switch until long after, myself. I ran down the hall to the janitor when I should have used the telephone. One's mind does unexpected things in an emergency. It was not until later that I remembered about the switch and fixed it."

"Too bad," Bill said. "If the bells had rung you might not have a broken arm, Fred. Tell me, have you any idea who tripped you?"

"No."

"From what Peacock has told me it was some time after the lights had gone out. What were you doing up there all that time?"

"I wasn't up there all that time. I sent out warnings and then returned here. This office, as Miss Conrad has said, was a madhouse for a few minutes. After something like order had been restored I returned to the second floor to get Miss Kelton's purse. She is the sewing teacher and she was uneasy about the purse which, in the excitement, she had left in the sewing-room."

"Perhaps protecting the bag was the reason for your broken arm," Bill suggested.

"No. I didn't have the bag when I fell. I made another trip upstairs."

"Why?" Trenton demanded.

"I went back to check."

"Check what?"

"When I went for the bag I had a number of things on my mind about the blackout. I hurried to the sewing-room, found the bag on the table and came back here. It was not until I returned here that I realized that something on the second floor had bothered me. I recalled that I thought I had heard low voices and movements. I went back to the sewing-room to make sure there was no one up there."

"What did you find?"

"I didn't find anyone. Whoever or whatever it was that made the noise had stopped."

"Why didn't you release Smead then?" Trenton asked.

"It never occurred to me."

"Did you see Marjorie Blake?" Percy asked.

"Marjorie Blake! No! Was she up there then?" Hewing was astonished.

"She must have been. She was having trouble with her dress form. I did not talk to her until after you had fallen. I'm simply assuming that she had not been downstairs until I saw her."

"I think you are right, Mr. Peacock," Miss Conrad said. "Miss Blake came in here, boiling mad, because the members of the class had left her up there alone."

"Then the Blake woman must have been up there at the time of the murder," Trenton stated categorically.

"Not necessarily," Percy interrupted. "The actual assault might have happened after she came down."

"If we could fix the time," Bill said.

"Perhaps I can help you," Percy offered.

"Go ahead," urged Trenton.

Percy recounted the things he had done between the time that the lights had gone out and Hewing tumbled down the stairs.

Bill had been making notations as Percy talked. When he had finished Bill said, "There was probably a lapse of fifteen minutes before Hewing fell."

"All of that," Percy agreed.

"Did you go up immediately after Hewing fell, Mr. Peacock?" Trenton asked.

"No. I helped with Hewing. I went up probably ten or fifteen minutes later."

"Ummm. A half-hour had elapsed then, from the time of the blackout to your discovery of the murder?"

"Yes, if we are assuming that Christopher's throat was cut before Hewing fell," Percy replied.

"Are you assuming that? And why?"

Percy turned to Hewing. "Do you have any enemies in the school? Was there anyone in the building tonight who might have wanted to cause you a personal injury?"

"No. At least I am unaware of such an enemy."

Percy turned to Trenton. "I can see no reason for Hewing's fall—unless the murderer wanted to distract attention from the upper floor."

"It's a good point," Trenton admitted.

"If that's true you were too late to save him, Percy," Bill suggested.

"That's what I've been thinking," Percy agreed.

"Which made the bang on your head unnecessary," Bill continued.

They gave Trenton the full details of Percy's experience.

"Very peculiar, very," Trenton muttered when they had finished.

"Are you all right now?" Hewing asked.

"Quite," Percy replied.

"He's in better shape than you are," Klip said. "You'd better go home, Hewing."

"If you don't mind, I'd rather stay," Hewing protested, but he seemed very tired and his protest was weak.

"You need rest," Klip insisted.

"I'll take him home," Miss Conrad offered.

"No." Hewing objected vehemently.

"Then go into the inner office and rest for ten or fifteen minutes," she suggested compassionately.

"If you don't rest, Hewing, I'll insist that you go home to bed," Dr. Klip warned. "You'd better do as you're told. I have the police here to back me up."

"I don't want to be a bother," Hewing sighed wearily. "I'll give up and go inside." He rose slowly and followed Miss Conrad into an inner office.

"I ought to have a blanket," she called back.

Mrs. Billings dropped one from under her arm, grunted as she stooped for it and then with surprising skill tossed it over the heads of the men into Miss Conrad's waiting arms.

When the door had closed behind Miss Conrad, Trenton turned to Gloria and demanded, "Why was Hewing both anxious and willing to protect you about the bell switch?"

"Why shouldn't he want to help me?" she asked.

"Why should your ex-husband accuse him of having a faculty meeting 'on purpose'? I believe those were the words the young lady used."

Fanny nodded quick agreement.

"Christopher was in a mood tonight," Gloria replied evenly.

"Did your ex-husband suspect that Hewing had a personal interest in you?" Trenton demanded.

"I never knew what my ex-husband was thinking," she answered ironically, but Trenton missed the irony in her voice.

"We will get nowhere by hedging," he cautioned. "Is

Hewing interested in you?"

"He asked me to marry him," Gloria answered with quiet dignity.

"Did Smead know it?"

"I don't see how he could have known it. I didn't know it myself until tonight."

"Do you mean to say that you did not know that Hewing was in love with you before tonight?" Trenton boomed.

"I did not. He has always been very nice to me but he is nice to all the members of the faculty."

"When did he ask you to marry him, before or after the murder?"

"Before school this evening. I came early to prepare for the examination." She looked challengingly at Trenton. "Does this have any bearing on the case? Since he and I were the only ones who knew about it, how could it possibly be connected with what happened later?"

"We don't know whether it's connected or not," Trenton said.

"But it's a private matter," she protested.

"Unfortunately murder isn't private," he reminded her. "I have no desire to pry into your personal life, but I must do so if I think it has any connection with the murder."

"I realize that."

"Are you the other man in the case?" Trenton demanded of Henry Graham, who had been very quiet throughout the investigation.

"I'm a friend of Gloria's," Henry replied.

"And you rowed with Smead this evening, didn't you?"

"The young lady, Miss Fanny Hayes, gave a most accurate description of what happened," Henry answered.

"Let's see. Smead hit you over the head with a splint, didn't he?"

"Yes."

"Where were you during those fifteen minutes from the time the blackout started until Hewing fell down the stairs?"

"I was not in the building. I knew nothing of Mr. Hewing's fall until just now."

"I suppose you have an alibi for your time?"

"Not all of it. No."

"Why not?"

"I have no witnesses to what I did between the time I left school, ran home to reassure my mother, who is an invalid, and then came back here."

"Didn't an air-raid warden try to stop you on either of these trips?" Trenton barked.

"No. There were crowds of people around and the wardens seemed pretty busy. No one stopped me."

"So you left an invalid alone during a raid to come back here?"

"Let me remind you that it was an alert, not a raid, and that I have a nurse in attendance," Henry returned curtly.

"Why did you come back here?"

"To help Mrs. Smead if she needed me."

Gloria turned and smiled gratefully at Henry.

"Why should she need you?"

"She has a great deal of equipment to put away."

"Oh, I see. Did you know that Hewing was in love with her?"

"I'm not in Mr. Hewing's confidence," Henry replied stiffly.

"Did you know that the Smeads had kissed and made up?"

"No."

Percy knew Graham was lying, and wondered why.

"Did you like Smead?" Trenton asked.

"Definitely not," Henry replied with feeling.

"Please, Mr. Trenton," Gloria put in impulsively, "it isn't fair to question these men as if you thought they were the murderers just because of me. I'm sure that neither Mr. Graham nor Mr. Hewing knew that I had agreed to go back to my ex-husband. I didn't know it myself until recess time, when Christopher and I decided to have another try at marriage."

"Did you tell anyone?"

Gloria hesitated, seemed hopelessly bewildered. "No," she said finally. "Certainly not!"

"Would you have gone away with him had he lived?" Trenton asked.

"No."

"Why not?"

"Because of what happened immediately after I promised to resume marriage with him. Ask Miss Hayes to repeat her story if you have forgotten!" she challenged bitterly.

Trenton shuddered at the suggestion. He thrust a slip of paper toward Gloria. "This was on Hewing's desk." He held it for her to read. She looked like a trapped animal. "Know what it means?" Trenton demanded.

Gloria did not answer. She bit her lips, looked helplessly about the room, then back at the slip of paper.

"It is a memorandum, probably Hewing's writing, and it says, 'Get new instructor for First Aid class,'" Trenton read. He moved to the desk, dropped the slip and turned to Gloria. "If you won't explain what the memorandum means I'm sure Hewing will."

"Don't disturb Hewing for a little while," Dr. Klip advised.

"This is murder," Trenton said gruffly.

"Please," Gloria begged. "Let him rest. I'll tell you."

"You can explain it?" Trenton fixed her with a lowering gaze.

"Yes, I told Mr. Hewing I was leaving the school."

"When did you tell him?"

"During recess time. Right after Christopher and I decided to—"

"Did you tell him your reason?"

"No," she said defiantly.

"But Hewing knew, didn't he?" Trenton insisted. "He knew that you were going back to your husband."

"I don't know what he thought."

"She's trying to protect Hewing," Percy perceived. "She's not helping herself or him. Doesn't she realize that Hewing is completely in the clear? Why does she do it?"

"We'll soon find out what Hewing thought," Trenton turned toward the door to the inner office.

"Why must you do this?" Gloria cried. "You are trying to make me, to make all of us, believe that Hewing killed him because of me." She struggled hard to keep the tears back.

"Did you kill him?" Trenton shot the question at her.

"No."

Her head was not tilted back defiantly as before, when she uttered that second, brief "No." There was no defiance as Gloria faced her persecutor with level look. That candid gaze should tell Trenton that she was defending herself with the only weapon available to her. That weapon was simple truth. Simple truth, however, did not impress Trenton. He proceeded brutally.

"Then we must suspect everyone with a possible motive. I'm not saying that Hewing killed him, but Hewing had a motive if he thought he was losing you. He admits having had the opportunity."

"Then who threw Fred Hewing downstairs?" Gloria demanded.

"You seem to have us there," Bill answered with a grin. "It must have been a couple of other fellows."

Trenton had been scowling at Bill because of the inter-

ruption but his face suddenly brightened. "A couple!" he
said. "Two people were working together. Why didn't we
think of that before? You hit something, Bill."

"I don't think so," Bill denied. "This was a one-man job."

"Or one-woman," Trenton said pointedly, his eyes on
Gloria.

VIII

"HE HAS CONCENTRATED his attention on Gloria. He thinks her motives are stronger than Hewing's," Percy reasoned silently. "The little lie she told to protect Hewing will be used against her."

He could understand Trenton's suspicions without agreeing with him, but there was nothing he could do at the moment to combat the conviction in Trenton's eyes. There had been nothing in the testimony itself to aid Gloria. It had all been blackly against her.

Gloria met Trenton's gaze fearlessly. Her eyes were steady. She refused to be intimidated by his implied accusation.

A policeman came in and whispered to Trenton, who moved to the far corner of the room to discuss the situation with his man.

Percy crossed to Gloria. "Don't let him bluff you," he warned.

"Do you think he is going to put me under arrest?"

"I doubt it, just yet."

"But you know he suspects me," she said evenly.

Fanny sidled up to them. "I didn't mean any harm. I'm sorry if what I said has been bad for you."

"Don't worry about it, Fanny," Gloria said graciously.

"But I did talk too much, I thought. . . ."

"You didn't think," Percy said. "I asked you to keep quiet."

"Oh, but Mr. Peacock, that was before Mr. Trenton asked me all those questions. I asked you, remember it, whether to tell about the ghost. And you said 'You might as well tell him everything, Gracie.' "

"Don't blame her," Gloria begged. "The information would have come out later anyhow. It's best to have it behind us."

"Goodness!" Fanny exclaimed. "What was that?"

A series of heart-breaking sobs answered her. They turned toward the door. They could see nothing, but the sounds continued, mounting in pitch. A harassed policeman appeared and cried, "She's in the auditorium and is getting hysterical."

Trenton and his man moved quickly through the door to be followed by the others. Mrs. Billings reaching into her kit trundled out. Gloria rose. Percy detained her. "Better stay here," he advised.

In a moment they were alone. "What am I to do?" she asked.

"Just sit tight and take it. I think Fanny has done you a favor by telling all she did. At first I was annoyed with her, but the information would have been drawn out piecemeal anyhow. It's better this way. We'll be able to clear you."

"How?"

"I don't know."

"You don't suspect me, do you?"

Her appeal was pathetic. "No, Gloria. I know you didn't kill him."

"How can you know that?"

"Because I know you. The one time when you might have killed him was the moment you saw Ruth in his arms just after you had promised to go away with him."

"If I had had a revolver I think I might have shot him then," she said quietly. "How did you know?"

"We, most of us, react in much the same way," he said. "When I saw him with her in his arms it seemed that he had destroyed all that made life worth living. I felt the impulse to kill and it frightened me. It lasted such a short time but it was horrible. The aftermath was almost as terrible. Suddenly after that first surge of rage, anger and despair I didn't seem to care any more. I didn't care." Her brow drew together in a troubled frown. "Did I ever really love Christopher?"

"I couldn't answer that," he said. "You are the only one who knows."

"Why was I suddenly bereft of all the emotional feeling I had ever had for him? Am I a shallow person, have I no real feelings?"

"Perhaps you realized your true feeling for him or, what is more likely, you suddenly became aware of Christopher and saw him as he really was rather than as the man you wanted him to be. You had made him a symbol of what you wanted love to be. *He* didn't let you down. You let yourself down. I'm glad you're free at last."

"Free! Will I ever be free?"

"Don't feel that way," he begged.

"How can I help it? I feel so cheap being forced to talk about the men who did or did not love me. It's so—" she broke off. "It makes me sound like a cheap flirt who spends all her time impressing men. Am I like that?"

"You know you are not. Those of us who know you, know it too. You happen to be a type men like. You're pretty, strictly feminine, have a warm responsive nature and, while you're efficient, you're not aggressively dominating. In other words men like you, respect your ability to do things, are charmed by your femininity, admire your good looks and want to possess and take care of you."

"My experience so far does not prove you are right," she murmured with a sad smile.

"Don't make the mistake of judging all men by Christopher," he warned. "He was not normal."

"I sometimes wonder who is."

"We must try to believe that we are," he comforted quickly.

"I'll try," she promised with an apprehensive glance toward the door.

The others were coming back from the hall. Trenton came first, was followed by Bill and a policeman, who deposited a square of cloth on a table. Klip and Mrs. Billings were leading Ruth Teale between them. Henry slipped in unobtrusively. Fanny bounced in, her eyes wide with interest.

Ruth's eyes were red from weeping. She walked unsteadily. Little gasping sobs punctuated her movements. They settled her into a chair, and she looked about the room. Her eyes went toward Percy, recoiled when he returned her gaze.

She puzzled him. She did not seem to be the same girl he had seen earlier in the evening. Even her mustard-colored dress looked different. The change in her bothered him. Whenever he looked in her direction he caught her glance. Why was she so interested in him? Why did she sit and stare? Why were her eyes filled with speculation?

Trenton was facing the group when the door behind him opened and Hewing came back into the room.

"You shouldn't be up, Fred," Bill protested. "The doctor said—"

"That you need rest and quiet," Klip cut in. "Why did you get up?"

"Because I can't rest with so much on my mind. The responsibility of all this is mine."

"We'll take care of the details," Trenton promised. "If you're not going home, sit down."

Miss Conrad was behind Hewing. She helped him into the chair at his desk, smiled at him reassuringly.

Trenton turned to Ruth, who had finally controlled her

sobbing. "Why were you in the auditorium just now?" he asked.

"Because I didn't think he should be left alone," she answered with a long-drawn gasp.

"Was it you who searched him, went through his clothes?" Trenton demanded.

"No."

"Who did?"

"I don't know what you mean."

"Someone put the lights out in the school, attacked the janitor and during the confusion searched Smead's body," Trenton explained.

"I wasn't there then," she said. "I just came back from home."

"Why did you come back?"

"Because no one seemed to care about him. They left him in there all alone. It didn't seem right to me so I came back to be with him."

Trenton turned to Bill. "You should have left a man to guard the body," he accused.

"I didn't have any men to guard anything," Bill replied.

"Then you should have done it yourself."

Percy saw Bill curb an impulse to make an angry retort. He compressed his lips, his eyes sparked for an instant, he shrugged and listened as Trenton questioned Ruth.

"You were in love with Smead, weren't you?" Trenton asked her bluntly.

"Yes."

"Did you know that he intended going back to his wife tonight?"

"I suspected it."

"Why?"

"Because I heard him say something to her about going away together immediately after school."

"When did he say that?"

"When we were tying him in the cafeteria."

"Did you see him after that?"

"Yes."

"When?"

"Upstairs. Just after the lights went out."

A ripple of excitement ran through the room. Even Trenton was startled by the frankness of her statement. "What were you doing up there?" he asked.

"I was part of the team. I was up there when the blackout came. I had gone down the corridor. I was hurt. Then I felt sorry for him alone there in the darkness, so I went back to him."

"Why didn't you unfasten him?"

"Because I wanted to talk to him."

"I can understand that, but why didn't you release him while you talked?"

"I tried but I was nervous and upset. I couldn't get the knots undone. I was angry too."

"Why?"

"Because he admitted to me that he was going away with his wife tonight."

"So you killed him," Trenton accused.

"No, I left him there."

"Do you realize your position, Miss Teale?" he demanded.

"Yes. If I had killed him I would not admit having been near him, would I?" she demanded.

Trenton did not answer her. He turned toward the table and opened the cloth which had been brought in, exposing an assortment of odds and ends of evidence.

Percy leaned over to get a better view of the display. A piece of two-by-four, the probable implement used to knock him out, dominated the assortment. There were other things: his broken flashlight, a small shiny object, Christopher's wallet, a small notebook, a triangular bandage and a bit of white which looked like paper.

"What about this?" Trenton picked up the shiny object and held it toward Klip. It was a razor-blade knife.

"This was undoubtedly the instrument of death," Klip replied as he studied the knife. "It was designed for pocket use. It has a handle which folds back to cover and protect the blade when it is not in use."

"You're sure it could have done the job?" Trenton asked.

"Easily."

"Shouldn't it be bloody?" Trenton asked.

"There are slight traces," Klip replied. "It was wiped on that." He indicated the smeared triangular bandage.

Trenton took the knife and held it toward Ruth. "Is this yours?"

"No. No." She shrank away from it.

"We're dealing with a cool customer," Trenton commented as he replaced the knife and again addressed Klip. "Why didn't Smead cry out?"

"I think something was held over his mouth," Klip answered. "His lips were bruised and there were traces of lint about his mouth when I examined him in the auditorium. That same bandage was probably used to gag him for the first few seconds after his throat was cut."

"Sounds like a thorough and very methodical person," Percy suggested.

"Just what type do you mean?" Trenton asked.

"A person accustomed to thinking of details, a person with a trained mind who thinks of everything. A school teacher. . . ." He stopped, wanting to cut his tongue out as he saw Trenton's face brighten.

"I've had the same idea, Peacock," he said with relish. "And this rather confirms our opinion, doesn't it?" He held the bit of white up for inspection. "It's a woman's handkerchief, as you can see. It carries the initial G and it is the perfume she uses." There was no question about whom he meant as he sniffed at the handkerchief. "Yes, it is the same scent, gardenia. This is yours, isn't it, Mrs. Smead?"

"Yes, it is mine," Gloria admitted.

"Where was it?" Percy asked quickly.

"With the body, on the stretcher," one of the policemen answered.

"I thought so," Percy said with satisfaction.

"Just what do you mean by that?" Trenton demanded.

"To be frank, I was afraid it had been found in the murder room. I'm very glad that it was not."

"And why, may I ask?"

"Because it would have been more incriminating if found there."

"It seems to me it is incriminating enough. What do you want . . . a picture of her doing the act?" he asked sarcastically.

"No," Percy replied. "It has no blood on it, has it?"

"None," Trenton admitted regretfully.

"And there is no blood on Mrs. Smead, is there?" Percy asked.

"You know there is none," Trenton was annoyed.

Percy turned to Klip. "Isn't it rather likely that the murderer would have some blood on him?"

Klip nodded slowly. "Quite likely, but not necessarily. However, I would rather suppose the murderer to be covered with blood just as you are," Klip replied.

Percy felt uncomfortable as their eyes turned toward him. Ruth studied him for a moment. She shuddered and looked away. He thought she was going to say something but she had no opportunity, for Trenton directed another question to Percy.

It was unexpected. "Just what are your connections with

Mrs. Smead?" he demanded.

"We are friends, have been for some time."

"You are not in love with her?" Trenton asked the question as if he could not believe that all men were not in love with Gloria.

"No."

"But you do have her confidence?"

"Yes, in a professional way."

"And you feel quite positive that she had nothing to do with this murder?"

"Yes."

"Do you have proof?"

"No."

"Then we'll have to depend on evidence, won't we?" Trenton asked with one of his annoying smiles.

"Yes. That's why I brought up the point of where the handkerchief was found. It is quite possible that she dropped it on the stretcher when she inspected the splints and bandages while we were still in the cafeteria. That's why I say I am glad that it was not found in the murder room."

"That doesn't prove anything," Trenton stated.

"That's my point. It doesn't necessarily prove that she was in the murder room. I know that she could have dropped the handkerchief on the stretcher when she bent over it."

"Did you see her drop it?"

"No."

"Well then, one guess is as good as another, isn't it?"

"I'm not guessing," Percy returned sharply. "I'm interested in facts, people, clues."

"So am I." Trenton turned to Gloria. "Is that knife yours?"

"No."

"We know that Miss Teale was with the victim; she admits it. You dropped your handkerchief, when?"

"I don't know."

"But you were with him up there in that room, weren't you?"

"Yes," Gloria said slowly, "I was up there."

Trenton beamed, his eyes danced. "Now we are beginning to get somewhere."

"She killed him," Ruth cried. "She killed him because she knew about me. I saw her up there. It's a good thing she told you because if she hadn't I would have told you, no matter what they might do to me."

"So it was you by the door?" Gloria asked rapidly. "Did you listen to our conversation?"

"No," Ruth cried. Her breath caught. She sobbed again.

"It's unfortunate that you did not," Gloria said calmly.

"Unfortunate for you?" Trenton cut in menacingly.

"May I ask a question?" Percy interrupted, very much upset by Gloria's admission. Now the point he had made about her handkerchief could be turned against her by Trenton.

"Go ahead," Trenton said.

"You had a conversation with Christopher in room 244 after the blackout?"

"Yes."

"It was dark in there. I will not ask you what you said, only what you did. Did you untie his hands?"

"No, I did not."

"Did you free his hands in any way?" Percy insisted.

"I did not."

"Were his hands free when you talked to him?"

"They were not."

"How do you know?" Trenton demanded.

"Because he asked me to release him, particularly mentioned his hands," she replied.

"But you left him tied, to be murdered?" Trenton accused.

"I didn't know he was going to be murdered," she declared.

"But he was an easy victim." Trenton swung toward Hewing. "Have you any idea who tripped you?"

"No."

"Too bad. Do you know where Mrs. Smead was at the time of your fall?"

"No, I do not. Why?"

Trenton did not answer him but turned to Percy. "Do you know where she was, Peacock?"

"Not exactly. She was somewhere in the lobby. We had been talking together about her decision not to go with Christopher tonight. I had just started off to release Christopher when Hewing hurtled down the stairs. Almost immediately Gloria was beside me in the darkness offering to go for a stretcher."

"How soon after?"

"I said almost immediately."

"Interesting, very interesting! She says herself that she was with the victim, that she was on the second floor." Trenton rocked back and forth from heel to toe.

"Look here," Hewing cried, "you talk and act as if you really thought Mrs. Smead were the murderer."

"I do think so," Trenton said heavily. "She had motive and now we can prove that she had the opportunity because she was up there. 'Almost immediately' does not constitute an alibi, Peacock," he sneered. "She has offered no alibi for the time Hewing fell. Perhaps she has an alibi to cover the time when Peacock was hit. Have you?" He shot at her.

"She was with me," Hewing cried.

"No, Fred, I was not," she denied quietly. "I left the auditorium immediately after Percy, don't you remember?"

Hewing looked at her gloomily for a moment.

"You knew about the light switch for the auditorium too,

didn't you, Mrs. Smead?" Trenton demanded.

"Yes," she admitted. "The faculty knew about that and the janitor mentioned it when we were in the hall outside his office."

"Exactly. It all fits in."

"Your case is purely circumstantial," Percy warned indignantly.

"But it all fits together so nicely," Trenton purred.

"You can't do this to her," Hewing protested violently.

"And why not?" Trenton asked. "What's to stop me?"

"I can." Hewing jumped from his chair and hurried across the space to the gate and Trenton.

"Please," Gloria cried. "Don't excite yourself. You mustn't."

Hewing faced Trenton defensively. "She didn't kill Smead, do you hear? She didn't kill him."

"If you are so sure that she didn't, perhaps you know who did?" Trenton replied.

"Yes," he shouted, "I know who killed him. I did."

Trenton laughed. Klip looked at Percy and tapped the side of his head, then looked toward Hewing, who seemed amazed at Trenton's laughter.

Klip stepped up to Hewing. "I told you to take it easy. You mustn't let go of yourself this way."

Bill came up and took Hewing's other arm. "We don't believe you, Fred. Sit down."

"But I did it," he protested loudly. "With that." He pointed toward the knife on the table. The blood vessels in his face stood out in angry cords. They looked as if they must burst.

"It's swell of you to want to help her but you must let us work out the case in our own way," Bill soothed.

"You're blind, stupid," Hewing cried, shaking himself free.

"Perhaps," Bill agreed quietly, "but your confession will only confuse us and it won't help her. We know you love her, but you're not helping her now. This confession of yours only makes her guilt seem more probable. It will make us feel that you actually believe that she did it and you are trying to save her."

"No, no, no!" he stormed. "That's *why* I did it, to save her."

"Sure!" Trenton agreed smoothly. "We understand. You killed Smead, then you tripped yourself down the stairs and while you were being nursed by several people in the auditorium you rushed up there and hit Peacock over the head. While you were at the hospital having your arm attended to, you hurried back here and assaulted the janitor, turned off the lights and rifled Smead's clothing. It's no use, Hewing. You can't save the lady that way."

Gloria moved up to him. "Please don't go on with it," she begged. "It was wonderful of you and I thank you from the bottom of my heart, but I didn't kill him and neither did you. If the police want to arrest me we can't stop them, but they will have to prove that I did it and they can never prove that because I did not. Please!" She put her hand forward until it rested just above his splinted arm. With his free hand he took her fingers and pressed them to his lips.

"Don't you believe me?" he asked, releasing her hand.

"Of course not! I can't permit such a sacrifice, so use- . lessly."

Hewing's face clouded. He realized, as they all did, that Gloria's speech was her way of telling him that she did not love him.

"They don't believe me," Hewing said hopelessly to Miss Conrad. "You believe me, don't you?"

"Yes," she answered quietly. "I believe you."

"See!" Hewing cried. "She believes me."

"She's humoring you," Trenton said mercilessly. "She doesn't want you to become ill. You're a sick man, Hewing. I'll send one of my men home with you."

"No. You don't believe me, I don't want anything from you. I'll go by myself." He faced them all. "You heard me. I confessed and you wouldn't believe me." He began to laugh, laughed hysterically.

Klip jumped forward and with Miss Conrad's help led him out into the lobby. His wild laughter floated back mockingly through the door.

IX

GLORIA'S EYES WERE moist as she looked out into the hall. She moved closer to Percy and whispered, "Go to him, tell him that you are going to fight for me, that you will find the murderer and set me free. Tell him not to worry."

"Any other message? Any hope for him?"

She shook her head slowly. "He knows there isn't. I explained it to him earlier, tried to make him understand it just now."

"Are you sure he does understand it," he insisted.

"Yes. How could he help it? Hurry, please!"

Percy ran through the lobby and down the steps to find Hewing arguing with Klip and Miss Conrad.

"You can't go home alone," Klip stated emphatically. "You're in no condition to drive."

"And I refuse to be babied," he argued violently. "I'll have to get along with one arm for a while and I might as well start now."

"Get in the car. I'm driving you home," Miss Conrad said firmly. "And no more nonsense. We've had enough for one night. Get in," she ordered.

He slid into the car without further protest. "Follow us, doctor, so you can bring me back here, please," she added, taking some of the crispness out of her voice.

Percy moved up beside the car to Hewing, who sat there in brooding silence. "I have a message for you from Gloria," he exclaimed. Hewing's face brightened. "She said not to worry. I'm going to work on the case for her. I'll get the culprit. She has great faith in me. She wanted you to know."

"Was there nothing else?" he asked eagerly.

"No. That was all. You know how grateful she is," Percy said.

"I don't want gratitude." His lips set in a firm line. "Go ahead, Miss Conrad," he ordered.

"Queer duck," Klip whispered as he stepped into his own car.

It was all too queer for Percy. He reviewed the recent developments as he mounted the steps. No wonder Gloria had been afraid. Too bad she had been up on the second floor after the blackout. He fully expected Trenton to arrest her that night. He even anticipated the morning headlines, which he supposed would read: "Ex-wife Held in Love Murder."

As he stepped through the door into the lobby Fanny ran toward him, grabbed his arm and tugged him off to one side. "I've got something important to tell you," she whispered.

"Some other time," he said.

"No. I must tell you now. You know when I said to Mr. Trenton I saw Mr. Hewing just before he fell down the stairs—"

"No," he corrected. "You did not say you saw Hewing, Fanny. You said you were upstairs when he fell."

Fanny flipped her shoulders. "Well, that's what I meant, anyway. I saw Mr. Hewing there just before he fell. That's why I hesitated and looked at you when Mr. Trenton asked me what I was going to say, remember?"

"Yes, I remember."

"Well, you don't know why I hesitated, do you?"

"No."

"Cat's eyes."

"Don't be silly now, Gracie, this is no time to play."

"I'm not playing, I want to tell you about what I didn't see."

Percy was going to ask her how that was possible but gave up the notion.

"I didn't see anyone there to trip him and I would have seen someone there if there had been someone there, I bet I would."

"Fanny, please. As remarkable as your eyes are—" he paused for emphasis. "Whoever tripped Hewing was lying on the floor or was crouched down. Don't be—"

"There you go, you think I'm a silly fool. All right. I'll solve this case myself. I have ideas." She released his arm and ran from the lobby toward the front entrance.

Percy stepped into the office and moved toward the table. He paused to look at the piece of two-by-four and was just about to pick it up when Bill said, "Don't touch it, please."

Percy withdrew his hand, but his eyes were held by the flecks of bluish fuzz which adhered to one side of the stick.

"What did you do to Fanny?" Percy asked idly, as he continued to study the thin strands of blue material which had been caught and held by the rough surface of the unplaned stick.

"She said she wanted to talk to you. Trenton told her she could go home if she wanted to. Didn't you see her in the lobby?"

"Yes. She's gone. She's going to solve the case herself."

"God help us," Bill grunted. "I thought she told us all she knew. She did see plenty."

"It's what she didn't see that has her upset now."

Bill grinned. "She's not as much of a nut as she seems, is she?"

"When is a nut not a nut?" Percy asked. "She says she didn't see anyone trip Hewing and when I told her the man was either flat on the floor or crouched down she was annoyed with me but I dare say she'll get over it." He pointed toward the piece of wood. "What color pants was Hewing wearing?"

"You've got me, pal. I forgot to look," Bill said. "Why?"

"That bluish stuff didn't come off my head, or did it?"

"You're talking like Fanny now. It is catching, isn't it? Do you think it was used to trip Hewing? It was found in the murder room, you know."

"I supposed it was. You might check it to see if there is any of my hair stuck to it. Want a sample?" He yanked a couple of hairs from the back of his head and winced. "The skull is still tender," he grinned.

"You'd better give it a rest," Bill advised.

"What's Trenton doing?"

"I don't know."

Miss Conrad entered the office and busied herself putting Hewing's things away. Trenton came out of the inner office. "Have you arrested Mrs. Smead?" Miss Conrad asked crisply.

"No."

"Are you going to?" she demanded.

"Why?" Trenton asked, his curiosity aroused.

"Mr. Hewing won't rest until he knows. He's in a mental state if I ever saw one. He wants to know, made me promise to call him. If you arrest her, he will get the best lawyer in town for her at once. I promised to call him back."

Dr. Klip came in and overheard Miss Conrad's remark. "I'm worried about Hewing too, Trenton. What are you going to do about Mrs. Smead?"

"I'm not going to arrest anybody tonight," Trenton announced loudly. "You may all go home but before you go leave your address and telephone number with my man, and," he added, "don't try to leave town."

There were sighs of relief and a general stir throughout the room.

"I'll call Mr. Hewing," Miss Conrad said as she began to

dial the number. "Now he'll get the rest he deserves."

Trenton said, "Dunning, you'd better go up to Smead's house and see what you can find. I'll be at the office for an hour or two if you should find anything interesting. If not, you can report to me in the morning."

"Okay," Bill glanced at Percy, an invitation in his eyes.

Percy nodded slightly to accept the unspoken invitation, then followed Ruth Teale to the lobby.

She glanced back, saw him coming and increased her pace. He ran to catch up with her. She stepped back as he said, "Just a moment, Ruth, please."

"What do you want?" she asked sulkily.

"I'd like you to answer a question. Just one."

"I've answered Trenton's questions, he's in charge of the case."

"Perhaps I know something that he doesn't know," he said.

"That goes for me too," she retorted.

"Trenton has been kind to you because at the moment he wants to think Gloria guilty."

"He seems to know what he is doing."

"But does he know what you were doing?" Percy asked pointedly.

For a moment she seemed to boil inwardly. There was a retort on her lips which she suppressed. She waited and then said, "I'm afraid. Perhaps you know why. At any rate I do not want to talk any more."

"My question may help you to prove your innocence," he told her.

She turned startled eyes on him. "Are you suggesting that you think that I'm—"

"I'm merely suggesting that you're a more than likely suspect under the circumstances. Trenton will get around to it eventually, when he realizes that he forgot to ask you something very important."

"What?" she gulped anxiously.

"Where were you from the time you talked to Christopher until I discovered him?"

"I—er—"

"You'd better tell me the truth," he warned.

"All right. I will. You know what I heard him say to her about going away after the class. When the excitement of the blackout had quieted down, I went back to him in that room and demanded an explanation. He just laughed at me, said I didn't understand men, said that I ought to know that he still loved me, that he always would, that Gloria and he were something entirely apart from our affair. Perhaps you can't understand what a statement like that means to a woman. It broke my heart, made me feel cheap and dirty. I cried and he laughed. I was mad enough to kill him but I didn't. I heard someone coming and got out of the room. I paused behind the door and listened. I did hear part of their conversation. I heard him tell Gloria that I was nothing but an interlude while he was trying to win her back, that I meant nothing to him, that he only felt he owed me a good-bye kiss. I didn't hear her answer. I couldn't take any more. I ran away then, ran to the far end of the building and sat on the window-sill for a long time, thinking."

"About what?"

"That I would like to kill him. That's why what happened seems so terrible." Her voice caught in a sob.

"Did you see anyone while you sat there?"

"No, you don't see much in the dark when you are crying and looking at yourself, wondering what kind of a person you are. As much as I hated him, I still loved him."

"I know what you mean, but you're all right, now. Don't worry. Would you like someone to go home with you?"

"No. I want to be alone."

"Then go ahead, and thank you for telling me this. It helps.

Say, what kind of dress did you wear earlier in the evening?"

"Black silk," she answered quickly.

"Thanks again. Good night."

Henry and Gloria came out of the office. Mrs. Billings followed them, her blankets rolled and tucked under her arms. "Good night," she said and moved toward Percy. She stopped, hitched the blankets and advised, "Better get some sleep. It's a mess, isn't it?"

"Getting messier," he said. "Good night, and thanks for reviving me."

"That was nothing. Sounds funny, doesn't it, but you know what I mean?"

"Can we give you a lift?" Gloria asked.

"Thanks," he said. "I'm going with Bill."

"You ought to rest," she advised.

"So should you. Try it," he suggested with a warm smile. "Don't worry."

She hurried away with Henry.

Five minutes later Percy and Bill were driving up the grade toward Christopher's house. "Did you mean what you said about not being in love with her?" Bill asked.

"Yes."

"How come?"

"Do you mean why don't I love her?" Percy asked.

"Yes, I guess so."

"I don't know. I sometimes think love is a question of chemistry."

"Chemistry?"

"Well, what happens when oxygen and hydrogen are united?"

"You get water," Bill said.

"People seem to me to be like that. In them there is something the equivalent of the molecule. When two people meet the molecules are attracted or repelled. When all the molecules unite then you have love. When just a few molecules are attracted you have friendship and when you have a repulsion you have dislike. You must realize that one's reactions to people are almost instantaneous."

"I know what you mean."

"You like Gloria, don't you?" Percy asked.

Bill turned, surprised by the question. "Sure. I liked her right off the bat."

"I thought so."

"But I don't guess she had any chemical reaction," Bill said with a wide grin.

"She has a great deal on her mind," Percy reminded him.

"And so have I," Bill said. "There's a man up there beside that eucalyptus tree. See him?"

Percy peered forward. Bill was right. In the grove just beyond Christopher's house a man's figure was outlined. Bill pulled on the brakes. "He's coming out," Percy said.

The man came into the road and moved toward them. "What are you doing here?" Bill asked, as he stepped from the car.

"I've been watching that house, wondering what to do. Will you be a witness for me?"

"Witness to what?" Bill asked crisply.

"My wife is in there," he said angrily.

"Now what would your wife be doing in there?" Bill demanded.

"If you knew the chap who lives there you wouldn't ask," the man replied icily.

"Who are you?" Bill demanded.

"Carter Twitchell."

Percy stepped forward. "I'm Peacock. Are you Mr. Twitchell, the oil man, whom I met at the club last week?"

"Yes. Say, I remember you."

"Are you sure your wife is in there?" Bill asked.

"I saw her going in. Look!" Twitchell pointed toward the house.

For a single instant they saw the beam of a flashlight sweep across a window from inside the house.

"What is she hunting for? Did she ever write letters to Smead?" Bill asked.

"I don't know. I knew nothing about this until Billings telephoned me about eight-thirty and told me that I'd better watch Smead and my wife."

"Billings?" Percy repeated. His mind ran back to the scene between Christopher and Billings earlier in the evening. "Why should Billings call to tell you such a thing?"

"He didn't say."

"Too bad he didn't," Bill commented. "Say, Twitchell, your wife can't be in there with Smead. Smead's dead. Murdered down at the school."

Twitchell's jaw dropped; his pale eyes grew round. He whistled, "Murdered! Smead murdered! How?"

"I'll tell you about that later," Bill exclaimed, impatiently moving toward the house. "Come along. If that's your wife in there we'll have to ask her a few questions."

"You are sure the person in there is your wife?" Percy insisted.

"Well, no." Twitchell backed down. "I tried to find her after Billings called me. I looked all over the estates for her, and called some of the people we have met. I started out to look for her. We live just up the road about a half a mile. As I was walking down here I saw a woman go into the house. She's the general build of Mrs. Twitchell."

"Since it is possible that you have made a mistake, we won't run the risk of letting the person get away. Take the rear door, will you, Perce, just in case she tries to bolt?"

It was an imitation adobe house, low and squat with a heavy red tile roof. A long porch ran across the front of the house. It was dark and had a foreboding air about it. Percy walked along the path toward the service entrance as Bill and Twitchell moved into the shadow of the porch.

Percy tried the rear door and was surprised to find it open. He stepped in and listened. It was quiet for a moment, then the front door squeaked on its hinges. Percy heard footsteps running. He heard a bang and a grunt of annoyed impatience. The steps were getting closer. A door swung open behind him and the next moment a woman crashed into him. He swung and caught her in his arms. Her flashlight fell to the floor with a dull crash and she let loose a blood-curdling yell.

Heavy footsteps pounded toward them and the next instant the lights were switched on. The woman was struggling and yelling with wild fury.

"Well, I'll be . . ." Bill exclaimed. It was Fanny, writhing and twisting in Percy's arms.

Her mouth stayed open in an interrupted cry, her flailing arms stopped. "Oh, hello!" She greeted them cordially. "For a moment I thought you must be the murderer."

X

THE THREE MEN watched her as she slid from Percy's arms and started to readjust her clothing. "Goodness, you gave me a fright. That's no way to come into a house, creeping along. It's spooky enough with him dead and all, without you—"

"That'll be enough of that," Bill interrupted. "Catch your breath, slow down and tell us why you came here, and leave out the double talk, if you can."

Fanny gave him a cajoling smile. "I was looking for clues, of course. There ought to be a reason why he was killed, and if we didn't find the reason down there then I thought maybe we'd find the reason here. It's very simple, isn't it, when you figure it that way?"

"And what did you find?" Bill asked.

"Nothing so far, but I'll help you look," she offered eagerly.

"You'll go home and mind your own business," Bill scolded.

"I forgot to tell you there was a girl here," she said.

"Since you came?"

"No. This afternoon or for supper. There's two of everything out in the den. There's lipstick on one of the napkins and a vanity case with the initial *T* on it. Whose name begins with a *T?*" she wondered. The three men exchanged glances. "Oh, I know," she bubbled. "Ruth Teale! Of course, and all the time I've been trying to think of names like Tessie, Thelma and—. There aren't many girls' names beginning with *T*, did you realize that?"

"Well, now that you know, I want you to forget all about

it, do you understand?" Bill commanded.

"You mean you don't want me to say anything to anyone, but you know I couldn't *forget* it. Oh! There's something I nearly forgot in the excitement. Someone telephoned him."

"Do you mean to say you answered his telephone?" Bill gasped.

"Sure. I thought it might be a clue."

"Was it?"

"I don't think so. It was a man and he wanted to know where Chris was. He didn't seem to be a bit surprised to have me answer the call."

"He probably knew Christopher," Percy commented meaningly.

"Good heavens, then he thought—" she gasped.

"Never mind what he thought," Bill cut in. "Did you tell him about Christopher?"

"No. I said he had gone out and the man said, 'Is he on his way down here?' and I said, 'I don't know where down here is,' so the man said 'Tell him to call me when he comes in. He'll know who called.' "

"How come you didn't tell the man that Christopher was dead?" Bill asked.

"Oh, he would have asked me a lot of questions. You know how people are, particularly about a murder, and besides, my father told me not to talk to strange men."

"Your father was right. He's also probably worried about you right this minute, so I'm going to send you home with Mr. Twitchell. I do *not* want you to tell him all you know, get me? Twitchell, do you mind seeing the young lady home? She's dynamite for us just at present."

Twitchell ungraciously murmured assent and swung through the service door.

Fanny lingered behind and leaned close to Bill. "What will I say if he asks me questions?"

"Play dumb."

"How can I? He knows that I know something on account of what you just said. Suppose he wants to know why I was in this house. My goodness! Suppose he thinks I'm one of the—. You know, like the woman who was here this afternoon. I don't want strange men to think I'm a loose woman."

"Listen. Remember what your father told you. Get going."

She slipped through the door. They watched her join Twitchell in the road. "Is she crazy or am I?" Bill asked.

"She's crazy like a fox," Percy said. "She's riding an idea. She's annoyed with me and I don't think she's exactly in love, with you at the moment."

"That's a relief," Bill sighed.

"I'll have to make my peace with her tomorrow and find out just what hunch she is playing."

"Don't you think it will be a waste of time?" Bill asked.

"I'm not so sure. She's fairly astute. Suppose we look at the den she talked about."

The den was at the rear of the house. "The kid was right," Bill grunted. "He had a dame in here for supper all right."

"Might have been yesterday," Percy suggested.

"No. This stuff is too fresh, and not bad," Bill remarked as he twisted a slice of ham into a roll and popped it into his mouth.

Percy moved over to the table and looked down at the place which had been occupied by the woman. "Fanny made a bad guess. It was Mrs. Twitchell who was here," he said.

"How do you know that?"

"If Ruth Teale had been here with him he would have taken her to school with him. Remember Fanny told us that he passed Ruth on the road."

"Right. Say, do you suppose that this Twitchell guy or Mrs. Twitchell . . . ?"

"No, I don't suppose anything of the kind. Twitchell was

too surprised when he heard of Christopher's death, too concerned about his wife. Billings is the person who interests me. He must have called Twitchell right after I talked to him tonight. He was mad enough to do anything and evidently he did it. I wonder why?"

"Suppose we ask Billings," Bill suggested.

They jumped as the telephone rang.

"Probably Trenton checking up on me," Bill said and reached for the instrument.

"Suppose it is the man who called before?" Percy suggested.

"What of it?"

"Let me have it." He took the receiver from the hook and stood quietly for a moment before he said, "Yes."

Bill watched him in amazement. Percy's voice had taken on a distinctly new quality as he said, "I've been busy."

"Why can't you leave dames alone and tend to business," the voice growled over the telephone. "You said you'd be in here about ten. We've had a bad run of luck and need cash. Did you collect from that Stevens guy?"

"No," Percy answered and winked at Bill.

"Look here, if you're double-crossing me you'll be sorry. He said he'd pay you tonight at the school. Why didn't you collect the four hundred?"

"He didn't have it," Percy said.

"Then why didn't you let me know?"

"How could I?" Percy said. "I'm dead. I was murdered at the school during the blackout."

"What the hell are you . . . ? Say, what's the idea?"

"You're on your own from now on." A huskiness had crept into Percy's voice.

They heard the click of the receiver at the other end of the line.

"What was the idea of the ghost stuff?" Bill asked.

"You'd like to know who the man is, wouldn't you?" Percy asked.

"Sure. We would."

"Then I think we will. He's going to do a lot of thinking in the next few minutes. He's going to check on Christopher's death."

"So what?"

"Then he'll act and we'll know who he is."

"What did you make out of his end of the conversation?" Bill asked.

"That Claude Stevens was supposed to pay Christopher four hundred dollars tonight."

"Now we're getting somewhere," Bill chuckled. "Stevens is the man who slapped Christopher before class because he was biting his wife's ear, isn't he?"

"If we are to believe Fanny."

"I believe that all right. And Stevens was the fellow who was tied up on the stretcher just outside the janitor's office. He's the one who wanted to get out and do his job as a warden."

"That's correct, according to what we have heard," Percy agreed.

"Do you think Stevens killed him?" Bill asked.

"I don't know. Four hundred dollars isn't generally considered a motive for a murder."

"It adds up if the guy you're supposed to pay it to bites your wife's ear," Bill mused. "As soon as I check through Smead's personal things we'll go see Mr. Stevens."

"That's a very good idea. We ought to learn the identity of the man on the telephone at Stevens' house."

"You think so?"

"I'm quite sure he'll be at the Stevenses'. Don't be any longer than necessary going over those things. I'd hate to miss the chap."

While Bill worked, sorting, discarding, keeping letters, notebooks and memorandums Percy thought about Billings, Billings' white hot anger and Mrs. Billings' concern when they had talked together after his injury. Mrs. Billings had something on her mind in relation to Billings and the murder. He recalled seeing the husband and wife in earnest conversation out in the road after the all-clear had sounded.

He glanced at his watch. "Hurry up, Bill," he urged.

"What's the rush?"

"I'd like to get to Stevens' house before our telephone friend gets there."

"You seem dead certain of that."

"The four hundred dollars seemed very important to the man. He may try to get it from Stevens. I think we ought to know the identity of the man who telephoned. He evidently knows a great deal about Christopher."

"Okay. There doesn't seem to be much here. Just the usual run of things and a book full of telephone numbers. I'm ready. Do you know the Stevenses' address?"

"It's up the hill, the other side of the golf course. I know the house."

"I'm ready. Put out the lights."

The Stevenses' house was dark as they approached. A rabbit hopped across the road and vanished into the shrubbery at the east end of the house. A neighbor's dog barked several times. From afar there was an answering bark and then quiet again.

The bell tingled through the house. They rang again. Finally there was movement from above and a voice from the balcony asked, "Who is it?"

"Police," Bill answered crisply.

They could hear a quick withdrawal and the muffled sound of voices.

"You know the line to take with the questions?" Percy whispered.

"Sure. If you think of anything, check. They're coming down," he whispered as a light showed through the fanlight.

The Stevenses in bathrobes and slippers came to the door. They were surprised to see Percy as he followed Bill.

"Peacock is helping me," Bill explained. "Now, first, have you had any telephone calls in the last half-hour?"

Their astonishment at what must be Bill's clairvoyance was answer enough.

"Who was it?" Bill asked.

"A friend," Claude replied.

"Is he coming for the four hundred dollars?"

"What four hundred dollars?" Nancy demanded shrilly.

"I don't know what you're talking about," Claude evaded.

"Oh, yes you do," Bill insisted. "You owed Smead four hundred dollars and you were supposed to pay him tonight. Did you do it?"

"No."

Nancy stepped forward. "Claude Stevens, you tell me about this money at once. The very idea. So that was why you told me to be nice to Christopher tonight, to kid him along. Using me, were you?"

Claude made no reply.

"And because I did what you told me you got mad and created a scene," she shrilled. "You made a fool of me!" She hurled the charge at him.

"You didn't have to go as far as you did," he snapped back hotly.

"Wait a minute, you two," Bill interrupted. "At the moment we are chiefly interested in this man on the telephone. Who is he?"

"I think he was Christopher's partner," Claude said slowly. He turned to Nancy. "Now don't get mad," he cautioned; "I lost four hundred dollars playing poker."

Nancy gasped.

Claude hurried on. "Christopher invited me down for a little game. The place is in Redondo. They run a Bingo game out in front and poker and roulette in the back."

"I thought they had stopped gambling in Redondo," Percy said.

"Don't be naïve," Nancy cried. "It sounds like it, doesn't it?" She swung toward Bill. "You're part of the police force —didn't you know this place was operating illegally?"

"My beat is over in this section," Bill said. "I don't know much about what goes on in Redondo."

"Somebody knew about it. Four hundred dollars!" She set her teeth hard and spoke through them. "You're not going to pay it, Claude Stevens. I'm not going to do without things, I'm not going to let you—" Fear flashed across her face. "*Did* you pay it, Claude?"

He hesitated an instant. "No, I didn't pay it. I was supposed to meet Christopher before the class started, but he wasn't waiting for me in the lobby. Later there were too many people about and then . . ."

"Then someone killed him," Bill said.

"Yes," Claude agreed.

"Why don't we put these lights out and go into a room which is less conspicuously seen from the street," Percy suggested. "If our man is coming we don't want to frighten him away."

"I hope I never see him," Nancy said as she led them down the hall to a small den which opened out onto the garden. She waited for them to file past and then switched off the lights in the front of the house.

"Tell me what you did tonight after the lights went out

down at the school, Mr. Stevens," Bill asked Claude, who was studiously avoiding Nancy's eyes.

"When I was freed from the bandages they had put on me, I started for my post."

"Where is that?"

"At the intersection of the two roads about a quarter of a mile down the hill from here."

"How did you get there?"

"I walked. I left the car for my wife."

"That's right." She corroborated.

"Did you go to your post immediately?"

"No. Things were in a mess near the school. Billings ordered me to help him. He's the senior warden. I did as I was told."

"How long did that take?"

"It was a long while before things quieted down."

"How long?"

"A half-hour, perhaps longer. I don't know."

"Did you know what had happened at the school?"

"Yes. Ruth told me when I met her talking with Billings in the schoolyard. She wanted to go home."

"That must have been thirty-five or forty minutes after the signal for the blackout," Percy suggested.

"I suppose so, I don't know."

"Then you were near the school at the time of the murder," Bill said.

"I must have been if he was killed soon after the lights went out," Claude admitted.

"You left the school as soon as Billings freed you, you said," Bill repeated.

"That's right."

"Did you go back in the building?"

"No."

"Did you have the money with you tonight?"

"Yes."

"You did!" Nancy cried. "Where is it now?"

"In my wallet upstairs."

"I'm going to get it and you're not going to pay it. You were robbed." She had jumped up and had started toward the door. She stopped. "Why, I can play a better game of poker than you can. You never were any good at it. Four hundred dollars. My God! What a sucker you were." The sharp tingling of the bell stopped her tirade. "It must be the man," she whispered. "Remember you're not going to pay him any money." She hurled the warning at Claude before she darted out.

"I didn't owe it to *him*," Claude reminded them lamely.

They heard Nancy's feet clattering on the stairs.

"Better open the door and bring him in here," Bill suggested.

"Good evening, gentlemen," the stranger said as he entered the room. He was brassy, sure of himself. He was well but flashily dressed. A gardenia was wilting in his buttonhole.

"My name is Peacock. I talked to you on the telephone from Smead's."

The man's mouth sagged open. "You what?"

"I talked to you from Smead's," Percy repeated.

"You talked to me." He spoke slowly as though measuring the words. At Percy's nod his face brightened, his assurance returned. "You sure fooled me. Had me guessing. For a minute I thought— Dawson is my name. When did they get Chris?"

"Know anything about it?" Bill asked.

"How could I? Dames is what did it. I told him to lay off but he was strong-minded about his women. Imagine a guy like him going to school. Does that give me a laugh? Goes to school to get bumped off. Who's the dame involved?"

"You and Smead were partners, weren't you?" Bill asked.

"That's right. He was the outside man and a good man, too, in our business. He had a way with him. Brought lots of good customers in." He looked directly at Claude and smiled.

"Know anything about a man named Twitchell?" Bill asked.

Dawson shook his head. "Oh, wait a minute! Chris brought him in one afternoon for a drink. Oil man, wasn't he?"

Bill nodded.

"He didn't play," Dawson's voice was tinged with regret.

"Outside of being your partner, what else did Christopher do?"

"He was in the insurance business. I thought everybody knew that," Dawson replied. "As a matter of fact, he was trying to impress this Twitchell man the day he brought him in, something about a very large policy."

"Did Smead sell Twitchell the policy?" Bill asked.

"I don't know. I wasn't interested in it. I'm interested in my end of the business; that's why I'm here."

"We know why you're here," Bill said.

"I don't owe you any money," Claude spoke up. "That loan was a personal matter between Christopher and myself."

"Don't rat on me," Dawson said sharply, "or you'll be sorry. You know you owed that money to the house."

"You heard him threaten me," Claude cried to Percy.

"Why, you—" Dawson started across the room toward Claude. Bill put out an arm and stopped him.

"Christopher paid it for me, said it was a personal matter between us, that he had the I.O.U.'s."

"Listen, piker, give me the money and I'll go home and get some shut-eye."

"Do you have the I.O.U.'s?" Nancy asked, running anxiously into the room.

"No. But he knows he owes me the money."

"And how do we know that a person like you wouldn't try—"

"Listen, Sister. I pay what I owe and that doesn't mean money alone, get me?"

"I won't pay you unless you produce the notes," Claude announced defiantly.

"Why not?"

"Because I won't let him." Nancy flatly endorsed her husband's statement.

"Keep out of this, Sister."

"Don't 'sister' me," she snapped.

"Where are the notes?" Bill asked.

"Chris had 'em."

"There were no such notes on him when we went through his clothes or his things at his house," Bill said.

"They must be at his house," Dawson insisted.

"Not unless there is a secret hiding place. Do you know of one?"

Dawson shook his head slowly. "Caught the murderer yet?" he asked.

"No."

"Why don't you put this Stevens rat through the ringer? He owed the dough, Chris is dead and there are no notes. What more do you want for a motive?" he asked in disgust, turned and strode through the hall and slammed the door behind him.

XI

As the echo of the slamming door faded Claude asked anxiously, "You don't think I killed him, do you?"

"We don't know who killed him," Bill responded cautiously. "That's why we're here. You had a motive and you had the opportunity. Of course, the fact that you told your wife to be nice to Smead lessens your motive a little, but it doesn't eliminate the fact that you slapped Smead. You were sore at him. You didn't want to pay the money. It sort of adds up."

"See what you've gotten me into," Claude accused Nancy.

"I got you . . . Well, how do you like that? Why, you weak-livered fool! You did this yourself," she shrilled at him.

"Wait a minute, you two," Bill interrupted. "Let me see the money."

There were twenty crisp, new twenty-dollar bills. Bill examined them carefully and returned them to Claude. "You're sure you didn't turn this money over to Smead?"

"How would I have it now, if I had?" Claude asked truculently.

"It could have been done," Bill rejoined. "One thing more," he said, "I'd like to see the clothes you wore tonight; bring them in here, please."

While Claude was gone Nancy, calmer now, asked, "Will he have to turn that money over to Christopher's estate?"

"If he owes it he ought to pay it," Bill said.

"He was robbed," she defended. "Why do they allow gambling places to exist right under our very noses?"

"That's a question I can't answer," Bill replied. "If people didn't want to gamble they wouldn't do business, would they?"

"Humph!" she snorted.

Claude came back, a pair of light blue slacks and a dark brown tweed sport coat over his arm. There was also a cream-yellow sport shirt.

"Where are your shoes?" Bill asked as he examined the clothing.

Claude dashed off to return with a pair of crepe-soled moccasins.

"Okay," Bill said as he deposited the shoes with the rest of the clothing. "I guess that's all for tonight. Better stay close to home tomorrow so that we can get in touch with you if we need you." At the door he turned and asked casually, "That was the clothing you wore tonight, wasn't it?"

"Yes. Ask Peacock," Claude retorted angrily.

"I'm sorry, Claude, but I didn't really notice what you wore," Percy said regretfully.

When they were once again in the car Bill asked, "What about our friend Claude?"

"He's worried. He's afraid, too. His relief at our departure was too obvious."

"He could have killed Smead," Bill said, "but, for some reason, I don't think he did."

"Why?"

"Just a hunch. What a case! He's the most likely suspect so far, after Gloria, and yet I don't think he did it. You know we're going to have one hell of a time about alibis, don't you? That blackout makes it impossible for anybody to prove exactly where he was at any given time."

"Why didn't you ask Claude what time he arrived home?" Percy asked.

"He could have lied about it. How would we know?"

"We wouldn't. I'm curious just the same."

"Why?"

"I don't know. There's something that bothers me. Was there an I.O.U. in Christopher's papers?"

"If there was I didn't see it."

"Perhaps we missed it at the house," Percy suggested.

"Or the murderer might have taken it—which sort of brings us back to Claude, doesn't it?"

"Why?"

"I don't know. You tell me."

"If Claude killed Christopher because of the four hundred dollars wouldn't he have taken the paper at the time of the murder? You don't think he killed him. Neither do I. If he did there would be blood on his clothes, if those were the clothes he wore."

"Always an 'if,' isn't there? There was mud on his shoes but that doesn't mean a thing. I wonder if they were the clothes."

"Perhaps we can find out. Ruth Teale went home and changed into a mustard-colored dress."

"She did?" Bill cried. "I didn't know that."

"It didn't seem important at the time I first realized she didn't have on the same dress she wore early in the evening. Trenton was too busy trying to prove Gloria guilty. We can check tomorrow."

"It may be burned up tomorrow. What do you think we can get out of Billings? We're almost there."

"One never knows. I'd like to know why Billings telephoned Twitchell, wouldn't you?"

"Sure, if it has anything to do with what happened."

It was Mrs. Billings who let them in. "I was expecting you," she said, almost with relief.

"Why?" Bill asked.

"Because Percy told me what Billings had said to him about—" She eyed Bill in his policeman's uniform and said,

"Sit down. I'll get Billings." She scuffed away, her robe dragging behind her on the floor.

Billings came, his face a sleepy mask. Mrs. Billings stood in the door watching the men anxiously.

"What about you, Twitchell and Smead?" Bill asked bluntly.

"Nothing," Billings replied. There was no expression whatsoever in his face.

"Why did you call Twitchell tonight and tell him to watch his wife and Christopher?" Bill demanded.

Billings was the perfect deadpan. Not a muscle moved.

"You didn't do that!" Mrs. Billings cried in protest.

"I did," Billings stated flatly. "I'm not proud of it, but I did it. He made me so mad with his talk of all being fair in love and war that I thought I'd give him a taste of his own medicine." He looked from his wife to Bill and waited.

"Suppose you tell us more about it," Bill suggested.

"Well, Twitchell has a big insurance proposition that I've been working on. It's the kind of policy an insurance man likes to get and right now it would have meant a lot to me."

"How much?"

"Twenty thousand dollars or more."

"A nice sum of money."

"Very nice," Billings agreed, with no more expression than he had displayed before. "Things were going all right until Smead horned in on the proposition. He had no more respect for a man's business than he did for his wife. I wouldn't have minded decent competition, but he went to work through Mrs. Twitchell. I sensed what was going on when I saw Mrs. Twitchell in his car one afternoon. I haven't been able to get to Twitchell, and I figured Smead was getting in his licks. He was doing that, all right, because tonight he told me casually, as if I didn't know anything about it, that he had about closed an insurance deal with Twitchell. Naturally I was sore and lit into him. He just laughed at me and pulled that line of his. The more I thought about it the madder I got and after I had a talk with the professor, who said Christopher was a moron, I decided I'd be a fool to let a moron put anything over on me. If I couldn't get that insurance by being decent, I decided I wouldn't let Smead get it because he was a louse. I called Twitchell. I told him who I was. I didn't try to do it in an underhanded way."

He struck a match, lit a cigarette and turned his attention to his wife.

"You shouldn't have done it, Billings," she sighed regretfully. "It might break up their home."

"I didn't say anything had gone on. I just told him to watch them because he didn't know Smead as well as the rest of us do."

"You telephoned him about eight-thirty, didn't you?" Bill asked.

"I guess so. It was right after I talked to the professor."

"You were in the advanced First Aid class, weren't you?"

"Yes, my wife made me go with her."

"Where were you when the blackout came?"

"We were still in the cafeteria. We were supposed to take our victim to the third floor and then pick up Smead in room 244 to carry him back to room 212."

"So you knew where Smead was?"

"I was judge of my team, so knew where he was supposed to be. None of us bothered about the examination after the lights went out. I was around the school for a while, then went to my post on the road. My station is down by the village square."

"You had Claude Stevens with you, didn't you?"

"Yes, for a while. As senior warden I kept him near the school because we were having too many violations. People just don't seem to have sense at a time like that. They all wanted to get into their cars and drive home. You know how it is—each man for himself. Until people forget themselves a little bit, we're not going to win this war."

"Or solve this case," Bill added.

"Could you furnish Claude with an alibi?" Percy asked.

"For part of the time. I suppose he was down there doing his duty. I don't see in the dark very well and so I can't be sure."

"How about your own time?" Bill queried.

"Same as Stevens'. There isn't anybody who knows where everybody was during the blackout."

"Did you go into the school building at all during the blackout?"

He turned his eyes toward Bill. "Yes, a couple of times. After the first mad rush to get away had quieted down, I went up to get a drink—that's when Hewing fell. Remember, I ordered them to turn off the flashlight? Another time I went up just for something to do."

"See or hear anything which might help us?"

"No. I didn't. I was hoping to see Christopher. I was feeling mean enough to want to tell him what I had done to queer his little deal. I felt like seeing him squirm."

"Anyone see you when you were in the building?"

"I don't know about that. I was sort of looking for my wife here but she was nowhere in sight."

"Humph!" contributed Mrs. Billings.

"It's true," he insisted. "I was wondering what you were doing."

"Did you know that Smead had been murdered?"

"Yes. I thought I saw a light in one of the upstairs rooms and went in to tell them to put it out. There were a lot of people in the hall when I got there and they told me that something terrible had happened, that Christopher had had his throat cut and Peacock had been knocked over the head."

"Did you tell Stevens about it?"

"No. There was so much excitement there in the dark that I returned to my post. Some time after that Ruth Teale came out and asked me if it would be all right for her to walk home. Just then Claude came up and said he thought he ought to leave the school and go to his own post. I told him to go ahead. Ruth was full of the murder and was so upset that she jabbered like a madwoman. I was worried at the state she was in, so told her to go on home as quickly as possible. I sent her off under Stevens' protection so that no other air-raid warden would stop her."

"Did you see her when she returned to the school?"

"No," put in Mrs. Billings. "I don't suppose anyone did, because she returned after the all-clear sounded. The first time any of us knew she was in the school was when that terrible sobbing came from the auditorium, don't you remember?"

"And you can't be sure of Claude's whereabouts prior to the time you heard about the murder?"

"No, I can't."

"Well, Perce, unless you have some questions to ask I think we'd better call it a night."

"Tell me about Ruth," Percy urged. "You say she was upset?"

"She'd been crying. She was upset all right, her voice shook so that I could hardly make out what she was saying. The murder was on her mind. She said she thought you had slit his throat, Professor."

"Now, Billings," Mrs. Billings cut in, "you've done enough gossiping for one night."

"It's not gossip," he denied hotly. "That's what she said."

"You don't have to repeat it if she did," she said tartly.

"You say she thought I had done it?" Percy asked, amazed.

"That's what she said."

"Did she say why she thought I had done it?"

"No, she didn't. As a matter of fact, she changed the subject quickly as if she were sorry she had said it. You know how people are when they blurt out something. Nine times out of ten they regret it before their voice has died away. She was like that. She asked us not to mention it."

"She was right; you should have kept still," Mrs. Billings scolded. She turned and scuffled down the hall.

"I'll catch hell the rest of the night," Billings said ruefully, "and the hell of it is, she's right."

"What do you think now?" Bill asked as they climbed into the car.

"I still don't know. Billings is such a deadpan you get nothing from him in the way of expression. We've talked to all the people who might have killed him for the reasons we know except Marjorie Blake."

"Can't we leave her until morning?" Bill asked.

"If I know Marjorie I think we'd better," Percy said with a grin.

"Out of the confusion can you make any guesses?"

"Unfortunately no, Bill. Why do you suppose Ruth Teale suggested that I had cut Christopher's throat? What would make her think or say a thing like that?"

"Excitement probably. We haven't helped your friend much, have we? It looks like arrest for Gloria in the morning. Trenton will do it, too, unless we dig up something."

"We've dug up plenty," Percy said, "but it gets us nowhere yet."

"What do you mean by yet? You've got some idea, haven't you?"

"Several notions," Percy said. "Nice word, 'notion,'—it can

mean any type of mental condition. I learned it on Cape Cod last summer."

"You don't want to tell me about them, do you?"

"Not yet, Bill. The notions are sort of fuzzy."

"Okay. Did you believe Billings?"

"Yes."

"So did I. Why do we think certain people are innocent? Are we on the wrong track altogether? Are we kidding ourselves about Gloria because we don't want to think she did it?"

"No. I'm sure she didn't. Let's call it a day, if you don't mind. My head, like my notions, is a bit fuzzy and it's beginning to throb."

"I'll take you home," Bill promised.

Just before he reached Percy's house he said, "How about going in to Redondo for some coffee?"

"Not tonight, Bill. You go ahead. Call me in the morning."

He stood for a moment watching the tail light rapidly diminish in size until it blinked out as the car swung round the curve. He watched for the glow of the headlights which would soon come into view as the car crossed the long bare stretch of the down slope toward Redondo.

The light cut across the horizon. He saw a lone sentry walking his post near the listening station. Percy mounted the stone steps slowly, stopped dead as he gazed upward. At first he thought his eyes were playing tricks on him. There could be no mistake. His eyes had not deceived him. Tiny sparks were swirling skyward into the night out of his chimney. Through the wide window he saw the unmistakable flicker of firelight against the wall opposite the fireplace.

A cold chill gripped him. Fear passed, to be followed by resentment against the unknown person who had entered his house uninvited, had taken the liberty of lighting a fire, was even now, friend or foe, waiting for him. His sudden pique gave way to a rationalizing thought. An enemy would not light a fire. It must be a friend. He hurried up the remaining steps and opened the front door.

XII

His front door had long been in need of a drop of oil. As it swung open it squeaked. After the squeak came a loud clatter. Percy paused, put his hand through the opening and found the switch. The lights flashed on. It was quiet within the room. He stepped inside.

On the couch a figure stirred, sat up, peered at him sleepily as she unwound herself from the afghan which she had used for a cover. It was Marjorie Blake. She looked from him to the door and said, "My little trick worked. I didn't want to be surprised."

She crossed to the door and lifted a brass plaque and a piece of kindling from the floor. "I propped it up with this," she explained.

"I'll put the plaque back where it belongs," he said and hung it in its accustomed place over the mantel.

"I thought you'd never come," she complained.

"If I had known you were here I'd have come sooner," he said.

"Don't try to be smart," she snapped. "How could you know I was here?"

"You win." He stood looking at her, taking in her disheveled appearance.

"I was cold. I had to light the fire, then I got sleepy, so I propped that brass plate near the door."

"You scared me out of a year's growth," he said with a smile. "You didn't, by any chance, make coffee, did you?"

"I made it on purpose," she smiled. "It's there on the hearth keeping warm, I hope. The cups are on the table."

"It was thoughtful of you, Marjorie. Just what I need. Have some?" He reached down to the hearth and carried the pot across to the table.

"I've had some. My cup is there on the stand." She brought his cup toward him. "Aren't you going to ask me why I'm here, don't you want to know?"

He poured the coffee. "I think I know." He avoided her gaze.

"How could you?"

"You're worried and a little afraid and you want advice."

"That's right on all three counts."

"You think you know something in connection with the murder and you don't know just what to do about it," he continued.

"Right again. I suppose you also know that you are out of cream for the coffee."

"Sorry. I never use it myself. I buy it only for guests. Why don't we sit down and be comfortable?" He moved over to the fire, threw a log on and then sat down on the couch facing her.

"Was my name brought up during the investigation?" she asked.

"Yes, the police will question you tomorrow."

"Today, you mean," she corrected. "It's late."

"So it is." He sipped his coffee, looked up at her and said, "Too bad you didn't have some bacon and eggs ready."

"It's all right for you to be casual, Percy, as if you were accustomed to this sort of thing. Perhaps you are but I'm not, so don't try to be amusing. I don't appreciate it."

"I'm sorry again."

"And don't be so damned polite. Why don't you ask me questions, help me to get started?"

"I've no idea what you want to say unless you know who killed Christopher."

"No, I do not."

"But you have some idea."

"Yes and no."

"That's typical of the case. What is on your mind?"

"Did you tell the police what I said about Christopher when I met you in the hall?"

"No. I mentioned the fact that you came down later than the others. I didn't think it was necessary to tell them what you said. Why were you so long up there, Marjorie?"

"You ought to know, you saw me in that damned contraption. I'll never try to save money that way again."

Percy made no effort to hide his smile.

"I want to tell you I was in a fix. You saw me all pasted up with paper."

He nodded. "I didn't wait long enough to examine you," he reminded her. "Tell me what happened up there."

"Well, to begin with, in case you don't know, I was having a dress form made. You put on a cotton undershirt and then stand for hours while other people paste strips of paper over your body. We were on the second layer when the news of the blackout came. Those nitwits ran off and left me standing there, practically helpless."

"I gathered that. Why didn't you call them back?"

"Call them back!" she scoffed. "They went as if the devil was after them."

"I know. I saw them running."

"But what you don't know is how one feels all strapped up with wet sticky paper. In the first place it's almost impossible to move because it comes down over the hips, well down. At first I didn't want to spoil the thing and fully expected that someone would remember me and come back and cut me out of the darned thing. No one came. I called and there was no answer. I opened the door into the hall and called but there was too much bustling about for them to hear me.

When I stopped I heard Christopher."

"He wanted help too."

"Yes, but I couldn't go as I was, practically nude—not that he would have minded," she added bitterly. "He said he was tied up and could not move but I wouldn't trust him. I went back and found an old sheet which they use to cover dresses and wrapped that around me. I went out into the hall and saw someone going into that room. I could see the dark outline of a person in the door. It was Ruth Teale. She was crying and accusing Christopher of having made a fool out of her. Of course, she made a fool out of herself, but that's beside the point. It was too intimate a scene for me to interrupt so I withdrew, planning to catch her when she came out. I went back into the fitting-room and fumbled around in the dark to find my knife because I knew I'd have to be cut out of the damned thing."

"A knife, you say?"

"Yes, one of those razor-blade gadgets. I use it for ripping seams."

"Oh."

"When I found my things Ruth had gone and Gloria was in there talking to him."

"It all checks," he said.

"I know nothing about that. It was even a more intimate scene than the other. He was telling Gloria that Ruth meant nothing to him, that Gloria was the only woman in his life, and all that sort of rot. I walked away again. I gave them time enough to thrash things out and went back and called Gloria, but she had gone."

"You're sure of that, Marjorie?"

"I didn't see her and she didn't answer me. I went in after Gloria had left."

"It's a nice point, remember it please for future reference."

"Christopher was still trussed up and asked me to untie him. But I was thinking of my own predicament and told him that I'd untie his hands if he'd cut off that nasty dress form. I bent down beside the stretcher and tried to untie his hands. The knot simply would not come free. I took the knife and cut the pesky thing. Then he asked me to get him out of the splints, but not me, not on your life, Percy! Alone with him in the dark, I wasn't trusting that man. That's why I insisted that he get me out of my strait-jacket before I released him from the splints."

"He lifted himself up on the stretcher," she went on, "and started to slit the form with the knife. Suddenly I was scared to death that he might cut me with that sharp knife, so I went back across the hall for my big shears."

"Did you see anyone beside Ruth and Gloria at all during that time?"

"Yes, just as I got to the door of the fitting-room I saw a man dimly outlined against the windows. I saw him move right up to the desk, take something and—"

"That was Hewing after Miss Kelton's bag."

"Well, I didn't know who it was and I didn't give a damn. I didn't want any more men to see me in the state I was in, so I rushed back to the classroom. I hugged the sheet closer around me, knelt beside Christopher and told him to go ahead and use the knife to cut me out of the messy thing."

"I thought you said you had some of the form on you when you left the school."

"I did. I want to tell you all this because, if I don't, you'll always be curious as to why I said what I did about him. If you have to tell the police that, all right, if you don't—if you don't—" Her large face flamed and she sputtered incoherently. "Percy—well—I'm big and all that—an old maid, too—and—and—" Suddenly she gathered herself together and the words spurted out indignantly. "But one thing I can tell you I am *not* and that's a pushover for such a filthy man as Christopher Smead."

"He got fresh?" Percy asked quietly.

"I'll say he did. I was so mad I was just shaking all over. I pulled away from him and slapped him square across the mouth. He dropped the knife and laughed. I bent to pick up the knife, fumbled around and couldn't find it in the dark, then I thought the hell with the knife, and ran away from that room where Christopher lay laughing and laughing. Percy, you can't imagine the mockery in that laughter. I meant what I said when I met you in the lobby. I hope right now that he rots in hell."

"It was an unfortunate experience," he said.

"If I had thought about it I could have slit his throat," she said. "But I didn't think about it and I didn't slit his throat."

"But your knife did," he told her quietly.

"That's what I was afraid of. Do you think I'll be accused of killing him?"

"You were up there while he was being killed," he said.

"How do you know that?"

"There is no other possibility."

"How will that affect me?"

"I don't know. You came down after we had taken Hewing into the auditorium. I was on my way to look for Christopher when you bumped into Fanny."

"That scatterbrain!"

"She saw you criss-crossing the upstairs hall."

"She did?"

"Yes, and regardless of what you think of her, her corroboration of your story will help you, if they suspect you. Of course," he added slowly, "we don't know what happened after you left Christopher. What did you do?"

"I went into a closet off the sewing-room, put on a light

and tried to get out of the damned form."

"Put on a light! How could you, the current was off?"

"I always carry a powerful flashlight. I used it, of course. In that little space it was as good as a bulb."

"Did you close the closet door?"

"Certainly, I'm not an exhibitionist."

"Then that's why Hewing didn't see or hear you," he said.

"Hewing?"

"Yes, he went back to check on things because he thought he heard someone while he was there for Miss Kelton's bag."

"If he had called or if I had heard him perhaps this would not have happened," she said.

"That's only a guess. Christopher might have been murdered by the time Hewing arrived."

"Good heavens! Do you mean to say I was within a few feet of the murderer all the time?"

"I'm sure of it; the closet saved you. Just where is the closet?"

"It's a black hole which opens out of the sewing-room."

"I was wondering why Hewing didn't see light under the door—if it's a black hole off the sewing-room that explains why he didn't see it." But—Percy got up and moved restlessly to the window—Billings had thought he saw a light from outdoors. That's why he'd made his second trip into the school building.

"Give me some more coffee," Marjorie demanded. "My blood is running cold at the very thought of being so close to the murderer."

"And I want you to be careful for a few days," he warned, handing her the fresh cup of coffee.

"You think I'm in danger?"

"Yes. The murderer is going to grow uneasy as the examination progresses."

"Good heavens! I'd better hide somewhere."

"You can't do that, it would make the police suspicious."

"I'm damned if I do and damned if I don't," she said bitterly. "If I stay home I may be killed, if I go away the police will hunt for me."

"There's a point I would like cleared," he said. "You came down a few minutes after Hewing fell. You came down again after the all-clear. What were you doing in the interval?"

"I tried to go home. The warden sent me back. I didn't go upstairs again. I sat in one of the empty rooms on the first floor because I was in no mood for the company of my fellow men. I was still boiling mad at those women for leaving me alone."

"You knew what had happened to Christopher before you left the school."

"Of course, but as I told you, I was mad and uncomfortable and afraid of taking cold. I didn't get all that damp stuff off. I guess I was too upset to be reasonable about it. Of all the contrary things to work on, wet paper pasted on cotton jersey is the worst."

"I don't think you'll need to worry about yourself in connection with the police," he assured her.

"Will I have to tell all the story, just as I told it to you?" she asked anxiously.

"Possibly not."

"It's very late. I'll go home. Thanks for listening to me. I feel better now." She stood up and replaced her coffee cup.

"Is that the dress you wore at school?"

"No. I wore a blue wool jersey to school."

"Dark blue?"

"Yes. Why?"

"Never mind now. Come, I'll take you home."

"I came under my own power, I'll go home the same way," she declared sturdily.

"I won't have you prowling about alone at this hour of the night. It will take but a few minutes in the car. Put your things on!"

She reached for her coat which was over the back of the sofa and cried in alarm, "What was that?"

He had heard it too. A sharp cracking sound like the snapping of a twig.

"Did you step on something?" he asked, looking down at the floor.

"You know very well I did not," she cried. "It was outside." She turned a fear-ridden glance toward the window.

They both listened, tense, keyed-up. A log rolled over, fell from the andirons. They jumped.

"We're tired and nervous," he said. "Worn out. It was nothing, a bird in one of the shrubs, a small branch falling from one of the sycamores. They do that, you know, because of the blight."

"Blight!" she scoffed. "Blight nothing. I've had the queerest feeling for the last ten minutes. I didn't say anything because I knew you'd laugh at me. Someone has been outside watching and listening and you can't make me believe any differently."

"Far be it from me to try," he said. "I had somewhat the same feeling myself. As a matter of fact, if you will remember, I got up and walked over to the window once."

"That's right, you did," she agreed. "Why didn't you say something?"

"I thought it was nerves and exhaustion. Come, I'll take you home now."

"I'm afraid," she said as she slipped into her coat.

"There's nothing to fear," he assured her. "If some prowler did listen he heard nothing, because we know nothing." He had reached over and had switched off the light as he talked. There was enough glow from the fire to light them to the door. He opened the door, stood aside for her to pass, pulled the door shut and turned his flash on the top steps.

Zing!

The sound and the crackling of splinted wood came almost simultaneously. They were repeated immediately. Percy dropped the flash as he tugged at Marjorie to pull her down to the level of the top step. "Crawl," he whispered, "and quickly." Two more shots passed over their heads.

"Stay flat," he cautioned, "until I get the door open. Crawl in. His aim is getting better."

She crawled through. "Don't stand up yet," he warned. He crept after her and kicked the door shut with his foot.

"Stay down while I draw the curtains."

"You're not going to light any lamps?" she cried in alarm.

"No, but I'll draw the curtains. Don't forget the light from the fireplace."

"What are you going to do now?" she asked after the last of the curtains had been drawn.

"Call the police." The dial was clicking as he spoke. "Damn," he growled after a moment. "The line is dead."

"What are we going to do?"

"I'll still call the police. Come with me and I'll show you. It's safe to stand now."

He led her to a small room at the end of a passage. He drew the curtains and lit a lamp.

"Is it safe to do that?" she asked anxiously.

"Quite. This room overlooks the sea. There is no place where a sniper could take a shot at us." He opened the double doors of a cupboard to reveal an elaborate short-wave set. She watched him with fascinated interest as he called, and called. She sighed with relief when she heard him say, "Peacock would like to speak to Dunning."

There was a short pause before he went on. "Bill, I'm ambushed at my house, telephone line is dead, a sniper has taken a shot at me. Can you come up?" After a moment of listening he smiled. He removed his head phones, replaced the speaker and turned off the dials. "They'll be right up," he promised.

"It's a miracle. Radio has always been a mystery to me, something beyond my comprehension—and this! Well, it's sheer magic to be able to talk to someone from a cupboard in this room. I just don't understand it."

"It would be a good thing for people like you to understand it. Radio is one of the things which has made the world small."

"I can't think of anything but the man out there who tried to kill us," she said, shivering.

"Why are you so sure it is a man? Remember that Ruth Teale is a skeet champion. Whoever it was who shot at us is afraid of us, fears we have information to be used against him—or her."

"I'd still like to go away and hide," she said.

"You'll have to be safe. We'll speak to Bill about that when he comes. We'll see you home safely, don't worry."

They went back into the living-room. Percy went to the window, pulled the curtain aside a fraction of an inch and peered out. "I think the police car is coming," he said. "I see a headlight over the road."

"Good! Say, Percy, do you have any bicarbonate in the house? I don't know whether it's nerves or the venison I had for dinner."

"Venison, whew! Where did you get venison?"

"Claude Stevens gave me a roast. He's quite a hunter, you know."

"No, I didn't know, or rather I didn't think of it. I don't go in for hunting myself, not that kind. Ruth Teale is a skeet champion and Claude is a deer hunter. That's a remarkable coincidence."

"What's so remarkable about it?" she demanded. "And do

you or don't you have bicarbonate?"

"In the kitchen over the sink. I think it will be safe to light the lights now. As for Claude and Ruth, I can't tell you about them at the moment. I'm not at all sure myself. Just an idea."

"Well, they didn't both kill him," she said. She moved, barged into a chair. "Damn this darkness!"

XIII

THE NEXT MORNING Percy wakened to a dull thudding. For a moment he thought it was in his head. As he began to function, however, he realized that the pounding was coming from the front of the house.

"All right, all right. I'm coming," he called as he crossed the living room. He remembered that he had made the same announcement to the telephone the evening before when it had drawn him in from the garden. The banging went on. He flung open the door and Fanny almost fell into his arms.

"I thought you were dead or something," she gasped. "Your telephone didn't answer, they said the line was dead and I thought maybe you were. I ought to be."

"Wait a minute, wait a minute," he interrupted. "That talk is too fast for me so early in the morning. It takes me a long while to get wound up."

"You look as if you'd just combed your hair with a vacuum cleaner. Of course, I know it's early but I was worried about you and I thought you ought to know and I didn't know whether to call the police or not, but here I am."

"Come in. What's on your mind?"

"For goodness' sake what happened to your door? Look at it!"

"Those were made by bullets, Fanny."

"Did somebody shoot at you, too?"

"Too!" he repeated. "Fanny, did . . . ?"

"Uh huh. Gave me an awful fright too. Teddy was killed."

"What?" he cried. "Teddy who?"

"Teddy Bear. My stuffed animal."

"Oh-h," he breathed.

"But if Teddy hadn't been on the bed instead of me I'd have been dead."

"When did this happen?" he asked.

"Last night, after I saw you. I was brushing my teeth when I heard a squeal from Teddy. Gave me a jump, it did."

"Now, Fanny, please."

"The bullet hit him right in his squeaker, honest it did. It's a good thing it wasn't my squeaker, wasn't it?"

"Tell me, and leave out the squeakers, please."

"Well, I was doing my teeth, as I told you, when it happened. I ran into the room. It was a long while before I realized what had happened."

"Did you call the police?"

"No. I wanted to tell you first but I couldn't get you on the telephone and then I decided that it might be a good idea if whoever did it thought I was dead. They'll get a surprise when they see me, won't they, and if they are surprised enough they may give themselves away. What do you think?"

"I don't know."

"A miss is as good as a mile, they say. I'm glad they didn't kill you, too, or we wouldn't be standing here talking, would we?"

"No. Come in. Excuse me until I get some clothes on."

"You haven't had your breakfast, or have you?" she asked eyeing the coffee cups.

"No, I haven't. They were left from last night."

She moved over and picked up the coffee pot and went toward the cups and saucers. "You and the policeman, I suppose. I think he's nice for a policeman."

"I think he's nice for any kind of man," Percy said.

"But it wasn't Bill, was it?" she pursued. "He doesn't use lipstick, does he? He's not that kind of a man, is he? I'm not asking you who it was because it's none of my business, so you just go ahead and have your shower and I'll make you some coffee."

"Don't bother."

"It's no bother, and I'll fix you some bacon and eggs if you have any. . . ."

"If we have any bacon and eggs we will have some bacon and eggs," he said.

"I always thought that sounded silly, didn't you? Of course, you can't have them if you don't have them, but I'll see what you have and I'll rustle something for you because I'd like some more coffee myself and don't be too long, because I've got to tell you why I came, but my mother says never talk to a man in the morning until he's had his coffee, but you don't look like such a bear, or are you? Anyway we've been talking, haven't we?"

Percy retreated, mimicking, "That's the kitchen over there with the sink and stove, in case you don't know what a kitchen is but, of course, if you cook you would know, or would you?"

"You play nice," she said. "Why haven't you ever married?"

"Remember what your mother told you," he advised, and ran.

She laughed. "Oh, that! I trust you, I think," she added to herself as she looked at the traces of lipstick on the rim of the cup. She shrugged and went toward the kitchen.

When Percy stepped from the shower he could hear Fanny clattering away in the kitchen. Over the rattle of pots and pans her thin voice was singing. He caught himself listening as he dressed, conscious that it was rather nice to have a woman singing in the house, a young woman doing housework and happy about it. That was the way a man was meant to live. He brushed his hair and carefully looked in the mirror for a moment. He was critical but not too severe with himself. As men come and go he knew he was well above the average for looks. Why then, if what they say is true, had no woman decided that he was her man? He believed in the old saying that woman proposes. He looked into the mirror again, wondering why no woman had as yet proposed to him.

"Yoo-hoo!" Fanny's voice floated down the hall. "The eggs are on."

He opened the door. "I'll be there in a minute."

"How do you like 'em," she shouted back. "You look like a three-minute egg."

"That's okay," he called back. "I don't look like an egg, though. Or do I? If a man looks like a three-minute egg, he must look like a pain in the neck to a woman."

A gay cloth covered the table in the breakfast nook. Sometime during her preparations Fanny had found time to run out and pick a few yellow marguerites. They were in a pale blue pottery bowl in the center of the table. The bacon was crisp, the coffee smelled like ambrosia. A pile of toast was crisp and golden brown. His morning paper was neatly folded at his place.

"Sit down," she ordered. "I'm breaking your eggs. I suppose you like lots of butter. I'll let you season them yourself." She brought the egg cup and placed it in front of him. "There isn't any cream, but perhaps you don't take cream. I found that homemade jelly. It looks good. I think I'll have some of that. There's your coffee. It smells good. Do you like it strong like that? I do. There!" She slid into the chair opposite him and smiled.

She had finished half a slice of toast when she said suddenly, "My goodness! I hope you don't have nosy neighbors."

"They're just normal people. Why?"

"Well, if they saw your visitor come in last night and then

see me go out this morning, if they didn't see me come in, then they will think that I've been here all night."

"Don't worry, your reputation is safe. They've gone north for a week."

"That's good. This is fun, isn't it?"

"It's very nice of you to do this for me. Everything is delicious. Did you have some other reason for coming other than the death of your teddy bear?"

"Yes. I still think that Mr. Hewing killed Christopher."

He leaned across the table and smiled indulgently. "Have you found some new evidence?"

She shook her head.

"But you still think he did it."

"Yes. He was in love with Gloria, she told him she was going away with Christopher, and so, to keep her from going he killed him."

"But Fanny, it doesn't make sense. Hewing was in the auditorium when I was bashed over the head. He was in the hospital when the lights went out and the janitor was knocked over the head. We know that definitely, even though you think there was no one at the top of the stairs to trip him."

"I know. It sort of spoils my theory, doesn't it? Now, if someone else had done the other things then it would make it very simple, wouldn't it?"

"It isn't simple any way you look at it, and it may get worse before it gets better."

"You mean another murder?"

"Yes. That's why I told you to be careful. I hope Twitchell doesn't talk about last night."

"He won't. Not after what his wife said to him."

"His wife?"

"Yes. She'd been to a party in town. At least that's what she said. We were walking along the road when her headlights spotted us. He stopped but I kept right on going. I heard her say that she couldn't go out for one night without his finding some hussy to consort with. She meant me."

Their conversation was cut short by the shrilling of a siren outside the house. A moment later heavy steps were heard coming up the steps.

"I'll bet it's that nice cop," she said. "I'll warm the coffee."

"Why aren't you sleeping?" Percy asked Bill as he opened the door.

"Short-handed. A lot of the boys have joined up. Do I smell coffee? Lead me to it."

"Come and get it," Fanny's voice invited.

"How I have misjudged you!" Bill said, as he gave Percy a gentle poke in the ribs. "It just goes to show that you never know what a man is doing. Now you're the last man in the world I'd expect to be running a harem."

"It's your friend Fanny," Percy whispered, "and she's an excellent cook."

After a second cup of coffee Bill sat back and sighed. "The boss has a new idea, at least he thinks it's a new idea. I gave it to him. He wants to reënact the crime at the school to-night."

"They do that all the time in books," Fanny jeered.

"Don't we know it?" Bill grinned. "But that's how it's going to be. It's my job to round up all the people in the First Aid class and see that they are at the school at seven-thirty. I've got a list. I suppose we can contact all these people."

"Oh, I know everybody in the class. I can take you to their houses too, if you want to talk to them personally," she offered eagerly.

"Better let Fanny help you. It will save time," Percy suggested. "While you're doing it you can check on a few things for me."

"What?" Bill asked.

"Remember that piece of two-by-four that you wouldn't let me touch?"

"It was the piece that socked you. There was some of your hair on it," Bill said.

"And what about the blue fuzz?" Percy asked.

"Wool," Bill replied. "Two shades of wool."

"Blue wool," Fanny considered thoughtfully, as she started to clear the table.

"Don't bother with the dishes," Percy protested.

"It's no bother. I can work and listen to you talk, if you don't go away from the table; if you do it will be a bother because then I'll have to work and try to listen too."

"We'll stay right here," Percy promised.

"Who was wearing a blue wool dress last night?" Bill asked.

"I did," was Fanny's unexpected reply. "I knelt on something hard when I went in to see Mr. Peacock. It must have been the stick."

"Is your dress light or dark?" Percy asked.

"You ought to know what color it was," she said. "You were with me enough. It's practically a robin's-egg blue but it isn't quite because—"

"Okay," Bill cut her off with a wink at Percy. "There was dark blue wool on the stick too."

"Dark blue," she repeated and stood meditatively before the sink, a cup in her hand. "Dark blue wool. Ruth Teale," she said after deliberation.

"Are you sure?" Percy asked.

"Of course I'm sure. Women aren't like men. They notice what other women wear. It was a dark blue knitted dress— she made it herself and it looked it."

"Meow," Bill teased.

"Maybe I am a cat but it's the truth. It looked as if she

knitted it on a pitch fork; it was all hummocks."

"I'll take your word for it," Bill grinned. "Do you knit too?"

She nodded. "Want me to make you a pair of socks?"

"Well . . ." Bill drawled.

"What size do you wear?" She looked down. "Umm, big feet. I'll do it right away because there'll probably be a shortage of wool the first thing you know. My father says we're going to be short of a lot of things. It wouldn't be any fun to be short of socks, would it, on a cold night?"

"Ruth changed her dress, didn't she?" Bill asked Percy.

"Yes, she went home and came back to the school later."

"We'd better get hold of that dress."

"Marjorie Blake wore a dark blue woolen dress too," Fanny interrupted. "I just remembered that."

Bill watched her for a moment before he asked, "Do women notice what men wear, Fanny?"

"Yes and no. If a man looks nice, you're not apt to remember whether it was a blue suit or a brown suit, but if he is all wrong the way Claude Stevens was last night, then you notice."

"What was wrong with Claude?" Percy asked.

"His tie. He wore a brown coat, blue slacks—light blue they were—a yellow shirt and a very bilious green tie. His wife ought to know better if she knows anything."

"You're sure?" Bill asked.

"Of course I'm sure. He wouldn't have looked so awful if he'd had a decent tie. Now Mr. Hewing always looks nice, so does Mr. Peacock."

"None of your flattery, Fanny," Percy said.

"You haven't called me Gracie once this morning," she laughed. "Why?"

"I don't believe Gracie can cook," he replied.

"Will you two stop," Bill cut in. "What was Hewing wearing last night?"

"Goodness, you ought to know. He had a dark blue sport coat, tweed it was. Hound's tooth they call the pattern, a pale blue shirt, dark blue tweed trousers and heavy brogues."

"Aren't you forgetting his tie?" Bill teased.

"It was dark blue or black. I don't remember. It was all right though."

"I guess we'll go into the clothing business," Percy said. "It would be a good idea to get Ruth's dress, Marjorie's dress, Stevens' slacks and Hewing's trousers for comparison."

"Why?" Fanny asked.

"Just an idea," Percy said.

"Do you want mine too?" she asked.

"We know about you," Percy said. "I left you downstairs. You didn't run up and hit me over the head, or did you?"

"You know I didn't," she said. "Why should I hit you over the head?"

"If we only knew why I was hit," Percy said.

"I thought we decided it was to make sure that Smead would die," Bill recalled.

"That's what we decided."

"There, the dishes are done. I hate to come into a house and see dirty dishes in the sink. I don't know who your girl friend was last night but I think she should have cleaned up the mess she made, coffee spilled all over, the bicarbonate of soda box left open to get damp and all."

"I have no secrets from Fanny," Percy explained to Bill. "She's very observant. She found lipstick on a cup and didn't think it belonged to you."

"Thanks, Fanny," Bill said.

"I was only fooling," she put in quickly. "Do you want me to help you with the list? I'd like to."

"Sure," he said. "We'll go up to the school and check, then get going."

"I'll meet you there."

"Be careful," Percy called after her as she darted away.

"She's a nice kid, if somewhat talkative," Bill said.

"Very nice," Percy agreed. "And she can cook too."

XIV

WHEN THEY REACHED the front door Fanny waved to them from the road.

"I'm sending a man over to get these bullets out of the door," Bill said. "It may help."

"Better have them dig one out of Fanny's teddy bear," Percy suggested and explained to Bill.

"For the love of Pete. Is she crazy, running about like this?"

"You figure it out," Percy said. "I can't. We'll have to keep an eye on her."

"What a job!"

"I learned a couple of things last night which may be useful to us. Claude Stevens and Ruth Teale are both excellent shots."

"Then that ought to let them out."

"Why?"

"I don't pride myself on my shooting, in fact I miss more than I bag but—" He looked from Percy to the door. "I wouldn't have missed you standing against this door. At least I'd have winged you or Marjorie. She's no sylph. I'd have punctured her somewhere. The person who took the shots at you was not a crack shot."

"It may have been a case of buck fever," Percy reminded him. "After all, in the gunner's mind there was a terrific hazard. Getting us meant safety and peace of mind to him."

"Why do you keep saying him?"

"Just for convenience," Percy replied.

"Let's get going before Fanny turns the school inside out," Bill said.

"I can't go. I have classes in an hour. In the excitement of what has been happening I forgot all about my job."

"Call the University and tell them you are being detained by the police," Bill ordered. "I'm making you a deputy."

"I don't think I'll word it just like that," Percy said. "The Dean isn't too interested in my passion for crime. He warned me that the publicity was not too desirable. It's too early to call him yet. I'll have to call from the village."

After several minutes of driving Percy asked, "Why did you suggest a reënactment of the crime?"

"You don't want Gloria arrested, do you?"

"Certainly not."

"I had to think of something to keep her out of jail. Trenton was all set to run her in this morning."

"Why?"

"Because he posted a man outside her house last night. She didn't come in until very late. Late enough for her to have been over here."

"Where was she? What did she do?"

"We don't know and she wouldn't tell. Closed up like a clam and refused to talk. When I told Trenton about the attempt on your life, about Marjorie being here, he decided that Gloria tried to polish you both off. He's a hard man to unconvince. He's sure that she thinks Marjorie can give her away."

"Rot!" Percy growled. "If the murderer has any sense at all, he will realize by now that neither Marjorie nor I nor Fanny know anything incriminating. For a time I was afraid there might be more killings, but I think we will be spared that."

"Does a hunted man have sense? Won't his fear of discovery move him to more and more desperate attempts to cover up?" Bill asked.

"He seems to be well covered. Or have you found out something?"

"Don't try to be funny so early in the morning. I have an idea I want to discuss with you."

"I'd like an idea," Percy said. "Who's your suspect?"

"Henry Graham."

"I've been thinking about him too."

"Good, then you'll understand what I mean. Trenton has been so anxious to pin the business on Gloria that he sloughed right over Graham."

"Right. What are your ideas about Henry?"

"Well, according to Fanny, he had a row with Smead and Christopher hit him over the head with a splint. That's enough to make any man fighting mad, especially when he's humiliated like that before a lot of other people. He was at the school. He says he ran home during the blackout, maybe he did—we can check that—but he came back to the school—to help Gloria put away her equipment, he says. He could have returned in time to do the job, bash you, hit the janitor, loot Smead's wallet, everything. How do we know that he didn't owe money to Smead also?"

"We don't, but it doesn't seem likely," Percy said.

"He's in love with Gloria, isn't he?" Bill asked.

"I understand that he has always been in love with her, was in love long before Christopher came on the scene."

"Well, then," Bill argued. "Why don't we look into Graham a little more? If he knew that she was going away with Smead I'd say that he was more than a slight suspect."

Percy considered a moment. He looked back as the car swung around curves and they climbed upward. Behind him was the view he loved: the tall yellow cliffs jutting out into the sea, the great curve of the shore northward, the white beach, the greenish blue of the water and the glistening ripple of foam from the breaking waves.

"Graham's been on my mind," he said slowly. "He did lie when Trenton questioned him about the Smead reconciliation last night. Henry saw them kiss, just as I did. He walked up the stairs afterwards like a whipped dog. Why do you suppose Graham said that he knew nothing about it?"

"I knew I was right."

"Don't jump at conclusions," Percy warned.

"What's the matter now?"

"Nothing. Henry Graham might possibly be the man we want. He is the quiet type. I've known Henry for a long time and know very little about him. He is devoted to this invalid mother."

"A mama's boy, eh?"

"Yes and no. There's a possibility of a psychological complication in Henry's life. He's not the sissy type, however. He has protected himself very well. He goes in for things, has many substitutions for what we would call a normal life. His life is not normal because of the way it has been limited by his mother's illness. You'll probably be interested to know that he has a gun room."

"Oh, boy!" Bill exclaimed. "It's beginning to make sense."

"You're forgetting that Christopher was not shot."

"But they tried to shoot you only last night," Bill retorted.

"Doesn't mean a thing unless we can prove that the bullets came from one of Henry's guns," Percy reminded him.

"How would you like to take a bet right now?" Bill asked. "I'll give you five to one that we'll find it was Graham's rifle which fired the shot."

"Are we betting on the rifle or on Graham?" Percy asked cagily.

"Both."

"If Graham fired the shots from his rifle I'll pay you five dollars. If Graham did not fire the shots but his gun was used then I'll settle with you for twelve fifty," Percy said.

"Why the cut rate?"

"I want to be fair," Percy said.

There were some curious people walking about the plaza in front of the school when Bill drove up and left his car in a "No Parking" area.

Fanny called cheerfully from the top of the steps.

"I'll wait outside while you're checking your list," Percy told Bill as he started up the stairs.

As soon as Bill and Fanny had disappeared inside, Percy turned away from the steps and crossed the grassy bank toward the windows of the principal's office. He had to walk carefully because the grass was wet and slippery. He moved up to the edge of the grass and walked carefully, looking at the wet soggy earth which rimmed the building. Near the far corner of the school he bent down quite satisfied. He had been right. There were footprints. They went in close to the building wall. He paralleled the marks which led him back toward the main entrance. About halfway down he found a double set of tracks. They were marks made by the same set of shoes. They ended at a square slab of concrete.

He followed the double set of tracks to the open windows, and pressed himself close to the building. It was quiet inside. After a moment he heard a voice say, "We have no right to open the night school locker, but I suppose we must do it. Don't disturb their things any more than you can help."

He heard Fanny's voice and Bill's low assurance that they would disturb nothing.

Satisfied that his hunch had been right, he left his listening post and returned to the top of the steps to wait for them.

"What on earth have you been doing?" Fanny asked when she spied his shoes.

"Walking on the good earth," he replied.

"You've ruined your shoes, or will you be able to clean them? What were you doing?"

"Exploring an idea."

"We've checked the list," Bill said.

"Why don't you give it to Fanny and let her go home and telephone all the people concerned to come here tonight?" Percy suggested.

"You're just doing that to get rid of me," she objected. "You've found something and you don't want me to know about it."

"Fanny, you amaze me. I don't want that pretty little head of yours all muddled up. Do as you're told for once, will you?" Percy urged.

"What else can I do? Telephoning a lot of people is no fun."

"It could be," Percy said. "You might learn a lot by the way they react to your message. Let me see the list a moment." He found Henry Graham's telephone number and handed the list back to Fanny. "Go ahead, and don't gossip. Just give them your message and ring off. Don't tell them anything else, please."

"Okay. Where will you be if I want you?" she asked.

"We'll keep in touch with you," he promised.

"What's on your mind?" Bill asked.

"Those clothes we mentioned, and now I want to inspect a couple of pairs of shoes."

He turned to Fanny and spoke with good-natured impatience. "Get along with you now, Fanny. Can't have you overhearing all our plans and purposes." Fanny went unwillingly down the steps.

"I thought so. Whose shoes?"

"Claude Stevens' and Henry Graham's. Someone was under the office window last night listening. I think the man who listened turned the lights out and attacked the janitor."

"But why Graham's shoes?"

"Because they were muddy. I noticed it when he sat next to Gloria but I didn't think it important then."

"Let's go."

"I must do some telephoning first. The University and

Graham's house. His mother is a sick woman. Let's give him a chance to prepare her for anything which might follow."

"The element of surprise is always good," Bill argued. "Why throw it away?"

"If he has anything to hide he'll be very busy from the time we call until we reach his house," Percy said as he went into the building.

After reporting his absence to the University he called the Graham residence. He waited several minutes before a low voice answered the call. He asked for Henry.

"Just a moment," the voice promised. There was another long wait before the same low voice asked, "Are you still there?"

"You'll have to speak louder," he said.

"I can't. I don't want Mrs. Graham to hear me. Mr. Graham is not here; his bed as not been slept in. Something has happened and I don't want to disturb his mother until I know something definite."

"I'm talking for the police," he said. "We'll be right up."

"Do you know anything about him?"

"No."

"I'll be watching for you. Be as quiet as you can," the voice begged.

Percy was in a deep study as he joined Bill.

"What's up?"

"I don't know." He told him about the situation at the Grahams'.

"I know," Bill said. "He's bolted, that's what he's done, made a get-away. I'd better send out an alarm for him."

"Let's go up there first. I know the house. As a matter of fact it's right next door to the place where we left Marjorie Blake last night."

They were winding up the curved road when the radio started to buzz.

Bill made a slight adjustment of the dial. "Calling car 49," the voice said.

"That's us. Trenton has probably thought of something new."

"Car 49 proceed at once to 22 La Venta Drive, Palos Rojos." The message was repeated. "A murder reported. That is all."

"Holy catfish!" Bill exploded. He stepped on the gas, the car lurched forward. "Why, that's . . ."

"Marjorie Blake's address. It's right next door to Henry Graham's place."

"What fools we were to put her right in his lap," Bill groaned.

"We didn't know. If we could only see into the future or properly read the past."

"What good would reading the past do?"

"We could have saved ourselves from a great many mistakes, this one for instance, Japan for another."

"It's all murder, isn't it?" Bill sighed. "I'll never forgive myself for putting that woman right where the murderer wanted her."

"She wanted to get home," Percy reminded him.

"Were there any other attempts made to get at you?"

"If there were I slept right through them after you dropped me off at the house."

"You'll need protection. I'd say there was more than an even chance that you're next. Watch your step, Percy, my friend."

As they parked in the road Percy saw the door of the Graham house open. A nurse was looking toward them expectantly. She came out and waved as they went up the walk of number twenty-two. She left the door slightly ajar and started running across the broad lawn toward them. The Graham property was about two feet higher than that of number twenty-two and was banked by a low brick wall.

The front door of twenty-two began to open slowly. "Look, Perce!" Bill cried. "Am I seeing things?"

"Marjorie!" Percy gasped.

"We thought—" Bill began.

"You thought that I had been—"

She didn't finish. A cry of shocked horror rang through the air.

"That's the nurse," Marjorie said and hurried forward. Her face was drained of all color, all her self-possession and assurance seemed to be gone.

She stepped past them, moving toward the wall where the nurse stood looking down into a stand of calla lilies.

"What is it? What has happened?" A thin, quavering voice called from the Graham house.

"Be careful!" Marjorie warned. "We didn't want his mother to know that he had been murdered."

"Graham murdered!" Bill gasped unbelievingly.

Marjorie pointed to the huddled form face down in the bed of lilies. "That is Henry Graham."

XV

THE NURSE WAS sobbing. Mrs. Graham's thin old voice from the window called pitifully. "I can't tell her. I can't, I can't," the nurse sobbed. "He was her life. Now she will die."

The suggested aftermath of the tragedy sent a cold chill through Percy, followed by a surge of hot anger.

"Is that you, Mr. Peacock?" The old voice took on an imperious quality. "If it is, will you send Miss Wilson back about her business?"

"You'd better go to her, Miss Wilson," Percy said.

"How can I face her? I'm afraid. She's so frail, the shock will probably kill her."

"Why not call your doctor and ask him to come at once?" he suggested. "Say nothing of what has happened until the doctor arrives."

"Will you come with me?" she pled.

"I'll follow you in a moment," he promised.

She turned and walked slowly toward the Graham house. "What is it? What has happened?" Mrs. Graham demanded from the upper window.

"Just something in the lily bed," Miss Wilson replied.

Behind him Bill was talking to Marjorie. "Who found him?" he asked.

"The dog and I." She shuddered. "The dog was acting queerly. I came out to see what was bothering him."

"How long ago?"

"Ten or fifteen minutes. I called you immediately."

"I think he's been dead a long time, several hours anyhow. Hear anything in the night, Miss Blake?"

"No. I was so tired I went to sleep at once." She turned to Percy. "You thought I had been killed, didn't you?"

"Yes," he replied slowly. "We thought Henry had killed you."

"Henry!" She gasped. "You thought that he—"

"Yes, we had just decided that he was the murderer."

"Of all the cock-eyed messes, this is it," Bill growled. "Why doesn't Trenton get here?"

Nurse Wilson appeared at a side door of the Graham house and called softly to Percy. "I promised her I'd go over," he said and stepped upon the low wall.

"The doctor's out," Miss Wilson whispered as he approached the porch. "Will you go up with me? I'll have to tell her. She's not easily fooled and she won't wait forever."

He followed her into the house. It was a semi-Spanish monstrosity, cold and impersonal. Their feet echoed through the tiled hall. They passed the dining room, stiff and unfriendly. For a fleeting instant Percy caught a glimpse of Henry's study as they passed the door. It was the one warm and friendly room in the house, in spite of the gun-rack opposite the door.

Miss Wilson ran ahead of him up the stairs. When he reached the landing she was standing at the bedroom door saying, "I've brought Mr. Peacock in to see you."

"To soften the blow, I suppose," Mrs. Graham replied as she extended a hand toward him.

She was pitifully thin. Her skin was tightly drawn over her bones as if to keep them from falling apart. There was so little of her that the wheel chair in which she sat seemed enormous. A woolen robe was thrown over her legs.

He took the slight hand and held it gently as he smiled at her.

"Why don't you tell me what has happened to Henry?" she asked.

"He's had an accident," he replied.

"He's dead, isn't he?" she asked.

His answer was a slight inclination of his head.

"I knew it had to be that," she said slowly. "He didn't come to me this morning. He didn't answer the bell when I rang for him. Poor Henry. How did he die?"

"We don't know yet," Percy replied. "They just found him a few minutes ago."

"What are the police doing here? Was Henry murdered?"

He was amazed at her calmness, startled by the directness of the question. "I'm quite sure he didn't kill himself," he assured her gently.

"Certainly not." She sipped some water from a glass Miss Wilson held ready. "What troubled him last night, Mr. Peacock, do you know?"

"No. Was he troubled?"

"Yes. He came running in soon after the blackout started, to reassure me that everything was all right but he didn't stay with me. He said he had to go back to get his car, but it was more than that. I lay awake for a long time, wondering and worrying about him until very late in the morning. He hadn't come in when I finally fell asleep. I was awakened by a noise next door. I heard voices and a car driving away. I must have dozed again because I wakened thinking I heard voices. I rang Henry's room and asked him if he had someone with him and he said no, but there must have been someone there."

"Did you recognize the voices?" he asked hopefully.

She studied him for a moment. He sensed a craftiness about her as she replied, "No. Now will you excuse me, please? I'm very tired."

"Would you like to get into bed?" Wilson asked.

"No. I'd like to be alone, to think things out. I'll call you if I need you."

He withdrew. Miss Wilson followed him a few seconds later. On the main floor he said, "May I have a look at his room, please? The police will come later but I'd like to look now."

"Go right in." As he stood making a mental inventory of the room she said, "I never thought she'd take it like this."

"She's a stoic," he said.

"She won't live a week, poor soul. He was her whole life."

"They were devoted to each other, were they not?"

"Oh, yes."

"Then do you think it is possible that in a time like this she might try to shield someone?"

"So you thought so too."

"Yes. I think she knows who was with him last night and won't tell us," he said.

"You'll never know unless she chooses to tell you," she warned. "She has a mind like iron."

"I gathered that." He moved over to the gun-rack. "Henry was quite a hunter, wasn't he?"

"Yes. It was about the only pleasure he had. He didn't go hunting this year, however, because she worried so while he was away." She came and stood beside him, looked at the rack a moment, pointed toward a pistol. "That's funny."

"Looks all right to me," he said.

"I don't mean that. It wasn't there last night, I'm sure of that."

"Perhaps he took it with him when he went back to the school."

"No. It has been gone for a week or more. I noticed the empty space one night when we were playing gin rummy and asked him about it. He said he had lent it to a friend."

"Did he say which friend?"

"No."

"Who were his friends?"

"You and Mr. Stevens were his best friends."

"Do you think Stevens had the gun?"

"I know nothing about it."

"But you feel sure it was not there last night? That point might be very important."

"I'm positive. I came down here to telephone the school after the alarm. This room is blacked out, so I had the light on. I was trying to get him. The line was busy. I tried over and over again. You know how your eyes and your mind work when you're trying to get a busy number. I found myself concentrating on the empty space, wondering who had the gun and what they were doing with it."

"Did you hear a shot last night?"

"No. I'm a very sound sleeper and never hear anything unless Mrs. Graham needs me and rings."

"You are tuned to bells," he suggested.

She nodded.

He moved close to the rack and sniffed at the muzzle of the gun.

"Do you think he was killed with his own gun?" she asked.

"This gun has been fired recently. I don't know how he was killed. Now if you'll excuse me, I'll go back to the police."

He went through the kitchen and service porch. He moved slowly, his eyes on the ground. When he arrived near the body, Trenton was superintending the police operations. Bill edged him away from the group. "It looks bad for Gloria again," he whispered. "Trenton thinks she came over here and killed Graham. Can't you make her tell us where she was? He's sore at both of us, keeps muttering something about following his own hunches."

"Let's not worry about that for a moment. Did you check on the bullets taken from my front door?"

"Sure, what do you want to know?"

"I was under the impression that they would be rifle bullets, but now I rather think they will be pistol bullets."

"They were pistol bullets," Bill agreed.

He told Bill about the automatic which had been restored

to its place in Henry's gun-rack.

"Holy cat!" Bill growled. "This case gets screwier and screwier. Are you suggesting that the gun which fired those shots at you belonged to Graham, that he was probably killed by his own gun?"

"Something like that," Percy replied, "and, oh yes, that you owe me just about twelve dollars and fifty cents."

"Not so fast. Graham might have fired those shots at you."

"Do you think it likely after his murder?"

"No. I'm just trying to hang onto the money a little longer, that's all."

"When are we going to take a look at Stevens' shoes and compare them with the impressions in the mud? Your men have taken impressions, haven't they?"

"Sure, that's been done. I'm afraid to go near Stevens now," Bill said. "Every time we think we have a good suspect we find him dead."

"Aren't you rushing things a bit?" Percy asked. "Graham has been our only real suspect so far."

"I know," Bill agreed, "but it seems like more."

"Dunning!" Trenton's voice boomed irritably. As they approached he gave Percy a grudging grunt of recognition and demanded peevishly, "Found any trace of the gun?"

Bill explained Percy's theory.

"A fine idea. What kind of a murderer do you think we have?"

"A clever one," Percy replied, "and a very careful one."

"What do you mean 'careful'?"

Percy gave him the detailed story of the automatic, its absence and unexpected return and the deductions he had made regarding it.

"Just fancy imagination," Trenton grumbled.

"Perhaps." Percy was amiable. "Yet reasonable."

"What's reasonable about it?" Trenton demanded.

"This," Percy began. "I believe that our murderer is afraid that one of the many people who were on the second floor last night may arrive at the truth. He is taking no chances. I believe that the murderer was prowling about these hills last night in an effort to cover his trail."

"So do I," Trenton snapped. "We know that Mrs. Smead was out. She will not tell us where she was or what she did while she was out."

Percy shrugged. "The murderer did one of two things. He tried to kill Fanny Hayes, then tracked Marjorie Blake to my house or went there to get me and, finding Marjorie there, tried to get us both."

"Why was the Blake woman at your house?"

"She was worried about the razor knife in the murder room, afraid that it was hers. It was."

"And all this business about the attempted murder of the Hayes girl!" Trenton snorted. "Mrs. Smead would naturally have it in for her, with the way she babbled all that stuff about kissing and the divorce and what not last night."

"Mrs. Smead completely understands Fanny and what you call her 'babbling,' " Percy told him firmly.

"I know you don't agree with me, Peacock, but I think we're wasting time. The one person with motive, opportunity and everything else is Mrs. Smead."

"I'm still convinced that she is innocent," Percy stated definitely.

"Then who is guilty?"

"I don't know. I'm completely baffled. There is no sensible pattern to this crime."

"Pattern," Trenton bellowed. "Don't stand there and tell me you can blueprint a crime."

"This second murder follows a pattern. The desire to cover up."

"As far as we know Graham was not near Smead last night

after the lights were put out," Trenton scoffed.

"True. I wasn't thinking of Smead. It's just a theory."

"What is it?"

"I may be wrong."

"Let me hear it."

"It has to do with the gun, Graham's gun. If we find that the bullet in Fanny's teddy bear, the bullets in my door and the one that killed Graham came from the same gun we do have something definite, don't we?"

"What?"

"I'm supposing that the murderer used Graham's gun earlier in the evening. When he realized that the bullets might be traced he decided to return the gun."

"But Graham knew who had his gun," Trenton protested.

"Of course he did. That is why Graham had to die. If the nurse hadn't noticed the empty space last night and the replacement of the gun this morning we would have had a pretty problem on our hands."

"We still have. We'll find out who had the gun."

"We can try," Percy agreed.

"Mrs. Smead could be the person who had the gun," Trenton said.

"It's quite possible, but I still doubt it."

"Why?"

"Because I believe Graham was killed in the service porch of his house and the body was dragged over here. There is every indication that something like that did occur. Come, I'll show you."

He skirted the area where Henry's body had been found. He indicated what he believed to be a track made by the body as it was pulled across the lawn. There was a smooth line across a newly dug flower bed and another spot of crumpled young plants. "His clothes were muddy, weren't they?" Percy asked.

Trenton admitted that they were.

"Hardly a job for a woman," Percy commented.

They went into the service porch. Percy pointed to what he thought was a spot of blood just inside the door.

Nurse Wilson opened the kitchen door. "There was someone in here with him last night," she announced. "They had cocoa. There are the cups and what's left of a chicken. Things haven't been cleaned up because the maid leaves Wednesday night and does not return until late tonight."

"How is Mrs. Graham?" Percy asked.

"Quiet now. I've sent for a friend."

"Where did you find the cups?" Trenton asked.

"There in the breakfast nook. I carried them out before I had my coffee."

He went into the breakfast nook. "I thought so," he said triumphantly. "Look at that." On the table against the wall there was a teacher's manual for First Aid work.

Bill shrugged at Percy.

"Well! What have you to say to that?" Trenton demanded. "So Mrs. Smead wouldn't tell us where she was last night. Good reason!" He was gleeful.

"It does look bad," Percy admitted.

"At last you're beginning to agree with me, eh?" Trenton declared smugly.

"No. I merely admitted that it looked bad."

"So does the lint I found on the door," Trenton said.

"Lint?" Percy repeated.

"Sure. Threads, probably came from that bandage under the books."

"Oh," Percy said.

Trenton was about to ask a question when Percy said, "Now there is something which might prove valuable." He pointed to definitely defined footprints on the linoleum. The impressions were brownish, mud-colored and crossed the kitchen toward the hall. "They lead toward Graham's room," he said.

"They're Graham's," Trenton replied. "He's wearing shoes like that—red rubber soles with little round suction holes in them. Doesn't mean a thing."

"But . . ." Percy started to protest but changed his mind.

The kitchen bell jangled over their heads. "That must be Mrs. Smead," Nurse Wilson announced.

"Who?" Trenton shouted.

"Mrs. Smead. Mrs. Graham wanted to see her. I asked her to come over. They've been friends for years."

"That makes it easy," Trenton said as Miss Wilson left.

"I wouldn't arrest her until after your little party at the school tonight," Percy advised.

"Why not?"

"Because I think you ought to discover the identity of the man who was under the office window last night. It may be important."

"Who was it?"

"I don't know."

"Did you see the prints in the mud at the school?"

Percy nodded.

"Are they similar to these?"

"No. Those at the school were made by a new pair of crepe-rubber soles."

"Oh." Trenton blew it out in exasperation.

XVI

When Gloria was questioned later in the morning she admitted that she had returned to the house with Henry for some hot cocoa. She also admitted that she had called the house earlier that morning and had been informed by the nurse that Henry had not been in all night. She had been puzzled, because she had left him there at home. She had been worried because there was no way of learning what had happened. She had decided to say nothing until she heard from Henry because she didn't want to get him into trouble.

"What kind of trouble?" Trenton demanded.

"Naturally, I didn't know," she said. "I couldn't imagine what had happened to him after I had left. He said he was going to bed."

"Did you see anyone when you left here?"

"No. I parked my car on the road. He had left his car in the village. At first he said he would ride down with me but he later decided to walk down this morning and pick up the car on his way to work."

"What time did you leave here?"

"I don't know. It was very late. We sat talking about the crime, exploring possibilities, eating chicken."

"We left Marjorie next door about a quarter of four," Bill said. "You must have left here before that. There was no car parked in the road when we came up."

"Perhaps it was your lights I saw as I neared the village," she said. "I didn't turn down toward the plaza but went along the upper road. I saw a car turn this way from the highway."

"It must have been us."

"You didn't get to your house until four-ten," Trenton stated after referring to a little book. "It couldn't take you twenty-five minutes to drive home from here."

"I stopped at the Stevenses'. There was a light in their breakfast room. They said they were getting over a visit from the police. They invited me to have a drink but since I had had chocolate here I did not stay."

"Dunning, were you at the Stevenses' last night?" Trenton asked accusingly.

"I haven't had time to tell you all that happened last night," Bill explained honestly.

"Since I'm in charge of the case it would be a good idea for you to find time," Trenton said testily. He turned back to Gloria. "Since you didn't stay at the Stevenses', what else detained you?"

"I was worried about Fred Hewing. I stopped at his house to see if he was all right."

"And was he?"

"I rang the bell once but, as there was no answer, I assumed that he was sleeping. I went home after that."

"You're a very considerate person, aren't you?" Trenton sneered.

"I've always tried to be," she replied gently.

"You realize, I hope," he said gruffly, "that you yourself are getting much more consideration at the moment than the facts seem to warrant."

"I know you think I'm guilty, if that's what you mean," she replied, looking him straight in the eyes.

"I do. I'm not arresting you yet but I warn you to make no further moves without letting me know where you go."

"I'll be here with Mrs. Graham until further notice," she promised.

"Be at the school tonight at seven-thirty," he warned. He turned away to have a long talk with Bill.

"Tell me how the Stevenses acted," Percy requested as he moved away with Gloria.

"They were fairly tight and very argumentative. They had something on their minds, for every so often, like a refrain, she would say, 'I think we should,' and he would say, 'I don't think we should.' "

"I wonder just what they meant," he mused.

"I've no idea."

"Why did you go to Hewing's?"

"I'm worried about him, Percy. He did try to take the blame for me, you know."

"Yes, I know he did. Greater love hath no man, and that sort of thing."

"Well—" she said slowly, "Fred's love isn't exactly that kind. He's more possessive, more jealous than sensitive to a woman's feelings."

"But he was taking a chance of being believed when he confessed," Percy objected.

"Did you believe his confession?" she asked.

"No."

"Neither did Trenton or Dunning. Perhaps it's horrible and ungrateful of me to say this—Fred has a—an objective, oh, almost a calculating mind—he's that way about everything. He knows what he is doing and why all the time. I don't mean to say that he didn't honestly want to help me, he did, but he knew perfectly well that his 'confession' would be a diversion and that Trenton would not take him seriously." She hesitated a moment. "I feel mean for saying this, Percy, but he's done everything a man could do to impress a woman with his gallantry."

"You don't love him and you refuse to be impressed?" he queried lightly.

"Yes, that's why I stopped there last night, to make him realize, if I could, that anything between us is out of the question. I don't want him to think, because Christopher is dead, that . . . You must think I'm a conceited fool," she apologized and color flamed in her cheeks, "running on this way about my love affairs when I made such a mess of my married life."

"Would you have married Henry?" he asked.

"I like him very much but I was never in love with him. He was nice, he never crowded me, never tried to make up my mind for me, perhaps if he had . . ." Her voice dwindled away.

"You wouldn't have changed, not while Christopher was alive," he stated and then repeated, "Not while Christopher was alive."

"Why did you say that in just that way?" she asked nervously. "You sound like Trenton."

"I will not say it in front of him." He smiled at her.

"You're wrong about me and Christopher. I did change, Percy. I was through with him before I knew he had been killed."

"I'm glad to hear you are sure of that. Otherwise you might have spent the rest of your life being in love with a phantom."

"You saved me from that," she said—softly, to keep Bill from hearing as he approached. "I'll go back to Mrs. Graham." She smiled at Bill. It was a warm smile. "I'll be here if you want me." It occurred suddenly to Percy that old Mrs. Graham's caginess might have arisen from her desire to protect Gloria.

Bill watched her for a moment then turned to Percy. "I've had my lecture on how an assistant to a chief should act. I'm a free man for a little while. What would you like to do?"

Percy referred to his watch. "It's after eleven-thirty and believe it or not, I'm hungry. Let's go down to the drug store. They put up a good lunch on Thursdays—you know, maid's day out and all that business. Half the community will be there. We might learn something."

"Sounds good to me," Bill agreed. "Let's go."

"Go the back way, over the hill and hit the highway beyond the Inn," Percy suggested. "The wind and the view may give us a fresh start on ideas."

"We need more than a fresh start. Trenton's sore at both of us, says we're trying to steal his thunder."

"Did he say any more about Gloria?"

"No, but I shouldn't be surprised if he arrested her any moment. He may not wait for the stunt tonight."

"Did he say we were to keep out of the investigation?"

"No. He doesn't want to admit it but he has a sneaking respect for your ideas. He realizes that he can't afford to make a mistake. He'll mark time for a little while anyhow."

They swung up over the hill and circled down toward the main road.

"It's hard to believe that we're at war on this bright April day, that this beautiful countryside may be ravaged by war."

"We can never let that happen," Bill said grimly. "They ought to let fellows like you and me get in right away."

"Our turn will come. It is an all-out war, we've got to educate our people to what that means first. When we all know it, then men of our age will have a place in the scheme of things, somewhere. It may not be what we would like to do but it will be important."

Bill swung the car over and cried angrily, "Did you see that crazy fool shoot out of that road? There's a stop sign too and he didn't even hesitate. He deserves a ticket."

"Wait," Percy said. "It's a delivery truck and I think it's on fire. See the smoke."

The truck was careening along the highway gaining momentum from the down grade. "I've got to catch him," Bill shouted. "It's a menace to all traffic."

He stepped on the gas, shot his car forward.

Suddenly the truck struck a chuck hole and veered off toward the left. Bill jammed on his brakes and slid to a stop as the truck went over the edge of the bank and rolled down the side hill. It rolled over and over several times before it came to a rocking pause upside down, its wheels spinning in the air. It was a light delivery truck. The rear door sprang open and a billow of smoke rolled up the bank.

They jumped from the car and were running toward the edge of the bank when a voice called, "Hey, my truck that I parked up there on that side road has disappeared. Have you seen anything of a light truck?"

A green-clad man was running toward them.

"You mean that?" Bill asked, pointing down.

"Yeah, that's it. How the hell did it get there?"

"Why don't you park so that your truck couldn't run wild over the highway?" Bill demanded.

"Cripes, it's on fire!" the man shouted. "How the hell did that happen?"

"This is a hell of a time to be asking questions. There's a fire station a few blocks away. I'll get the apparatus out here," Bill shouted and jumped into the car and zoomed away.

The man stood on the bank beside Percy. "Beats me," he said. "I'm a careful parker, especially on these hills. Of course, there are times when the brakes are not too good but I always leave her in gear."

"It's the exception which proves the rule," Percy said. "Perhaps we can save some of your load."

"Not a chance, look at her blaze! The tank must be on fire."

"What was your load?"

"I drive for the Excelsior Laundry and Cleaners at Redondo. There's a lot of stuff there that won't get washed this week." He took a pencil from his ear and rubbed the back of his head with it. "I *know* I put her in gear. The ignition was turned off. How do you suppose she caught on fire?"

"She was on fire when she rolled out of that side road."

"I don't see how that could happen," the man objected.

"Do you smoke?"

"Sure."

"Perhaps you dropped a lighted cigarette in one of the bundles."

The man refused to admit the possibility.

"I burned out the back of a sedan once with a cigarette stub I thought I had thrown out of the window," Percy said.

"Could be, but I don't see how. I've been wondering. Some kids put sugar in my tank once and made a mess of my motor. Do you suppose . . . ? No. There are no kids old enough for this job in the neighborhood. Look at her burn! I smell gas all right."

Bill and the fire apparatus came screeching back. The firemen jumped from their truck and started down the side hill with fire extinguishers. The tank exploded.

"There she goes!" the driver shouted. The next moment he yelled, "Look out!" He was not quick enough. He tried to yank Percy to one side but too late. A burning piece of laundry bag landed on Percy's shoulder close to his neck. His hair started to singe. With frantic haste he tried to brush it off. It stuck. He had to take hold of the burning rag with his fingers to yank it loose. He used his hands to make sure that his hair had stopped burning. The rag dropped at his feet and caught in the dry grass.

"Cripes!" the driver cried. "We've got to get out of here. Remember that brush fire in the arroyo a few years ago? Come on or we'll be trapped."

Even the firemen were scrambling up the bank of the hill toward the highway and safety. The grass, tumbleweed and brush were blazing in a dozen places.

Percy's hand began to smart. He wrapped his handkerchief

over his fingers to keep the air away from the burn, and called Bill.

"Hop in," Bill said. "I'll take you in to Dr. Klip."

There was no nurse in attendance as they entered Klip's office. Bill opened the door into the treatment room and said, "I've got another patient for you, Doc. Why, hello, Hewing. How are you doing?"

Hewing was having his cut hand bandaged. "I'm all right," he said looking out into the office. "Who's the patient? Oh, it's Peacock."

"Come in, Peacock," Klip called. "I'm about through with Hewing." He applied a dressing to Fred's cut palm and started bandaging. "Lucky for you, Hewing, it was such a nice clean cut. It'll be all right for a couple of days now. Remember, don't try to use that arm of yours. It would be fine if you'd stay in bed for a couple of days. You're all shot. Didn't those pills make you sleep last night? You look terrible."

Hewing smiled at Bill and Percy. "Cheerful for a doctor, isn't he? Of course I slept. Those pills knocked me out. I didn't know a thing until this morning." He made way for Percy. "Your turn."

"Take it easy," Klip flung after him as he left the office.

"I can't fly with one wing," Hewing called back.

"I'm going back to the fire," Bill said. "I'll meet you at the drug store in half an hour."

They discussed the fire as Klip worked on Percy's fingers.

"How's the murder coming, make any sense out of it, common or otherwise?" Klip asked.

"No."

"I understand you were there when they found Graham."

"Yes."

"The old lady surprises me. I'd have expected the shock to kill her but she's made of stern stuff. She's seeing to everything. The nurse tells me that Gloria Smead is the only woman the old lady thought was even half good enough for Henry." He finished the bandage. "Come back in a couple of days. You'll be all right."

"Did you know Henry very well?" Percy asked.

"In a general way. I was up there a lot to see his mother. Henry and I would have a drink together occasionally and chat. No better than that. Why?"

"I'd like to know who borrowed one of his pistols," Percy said.

"Sorry, I can't help you there. Doesn't your friend Dunning know? Henry often went to the police pistol range."

"No, he doesn't know anything about this particular pistol. I wish I did."

"There's talk in the village," Klip announced as he helped Percy with his coat, "but I don't think Gloria did it. Trenton does though." He looked at Percy intently. "I think it was an intimate job."

"What do you mean by that?"

"Henry didn't expect to be shot any more than Smead expected to have his throat cut. The murderer is someone they both trusted. Hewing and I were talking about it before you came in. He's all shaken up about it. Poor devil, he's worried about Gloria. He'd cut off his right hand for her."

"I don't think he helped her any last night," Percy pointed out. "As a matter of fact, I think his confession made Trenton feel more positive than ever about Gloria's guilt. He thinks Hewing is hiding something to help Gloria."

"I think you have something there," Klip acquiesced.

XVII

THEY WERE FINISHING their coffee at the drug store when Percy asked, "How long would it take your men to check the wool found on that piece of two-by-four with the clothing you picked up?"

Bill snapped his fingers. "Darn it! I forgot all about those clothes."

"Why don't we pick them up ourselves?" Percy suggested. "If we do, do you think you can get an answer back by seven-thirty?"

"Sure. Let's go. Where do you want to go first?"

"I'll call Marjorie and ask her how we can get hold of her dress, that is if you'll dial her number for me. I can't do it myself, thanks to these bandages."

Bill dialed the number and went to the car to wait. "She left the dress in the chest on her front porch for the cleaner to pick up," Percy explained when he came out. "It's probably gone now. We'll go by her house on the off chance that it hasn't been collected. It's on the way up to Ruth Teale's anyhow."

The chest on Marjorie's porch was empty.

They found Ruth in her garden working over a new bed of young plants. She looked up as they walked across the lawn and said stiffly, "I got your message. I'll be there."

"Oh, Fanny," Bill grinned.

"Yes, Fanny, and why anyone would trust that rattlebrain with such important work I can't understand. Do you know what she told me? She said Henry Graham had been murdered."

"He was," Bill said bluntly.

"How awful! His poor mother! Is there someone with her?"

"The nurse and Gloria."

"Gloria!" she repeated in surprise.

"Why not?"

"Well, since she's the chief suspect it hardly seems well, decent, if you know what I mean."

"We know what you mean all right," Bill said quietly. "But she isn't the only suspect, you know."

Ruth flushed deeply. "Meaning me?"

"Yes, meaning you. What did you do last night after you finally left the school?"

"I came home and went to bed."

"You can prove that, I hope," he said.

"Hardly, since I happen to sleep alone," she retorted.

Bill was slightly embarrassed, but after a moment he said, "We want to know why you ran home last night, changed your dress and then went back to school."

"I came home because I was horrified by what had happened. I wanted to be alone because I knew what some people would say. When I thought of him alone with no friends I decided to go back. I simply put on another dress, that's all."

Her answer had been quick, almost too glib to be convincing. It sounded as if she had rehearsed it.

"We'd like to see the dress you wore at school the first time," Bill said.

"You are looking at it right now," she cried defiantly, pulling at the neck of the dress. "It's the dress I have on this minute."

It was a dark blue wool dress. Percy chuckled to himself as he recognized the aptness of Fanny's description. "It looked," Fanny had said, "as if she knitted it on a pitchfork; it was all hummocks." Certainly, even to his unobservant masculine eye, the uneven rows, the knots and pulled threads on Ruth's dress proclaimed that she was no skillful knitter. Blue wool, boggled in the knitting, but—

"You told me last night that you wore a black silk jersey before you changed into the mustard-colored dress. Why did you tell me that?"

Ruth colored but she managed to convey nonchalance by a quick shrug of her shoulders. "I was upset," she said. "I did not remember what I'd had on. I thought, for the moment, that it was my black silk jersey."

Then she fixed Percy with a direct glance.

"What did you do with *your* clothes?" Ruth asked Percy sharply.

"I'm afraid they're in a disorderly heap in my dressing-room. Why?"

"I was just wondering," she replied.

"Did you know Graham well?" Bill asked.

"As well as most people."

"Ever talk guns with him?"

"Not often. He was a game hunter. My interest has always been in trap shooting and birds."

"Ever swap guns with him?"

"Certainly not. I wouldn't lend my guns any more than I would my tooth brush."

"I was just asking," he said. "Graham was shot, you know."

"Not with a shot gun!" she cried.

"No. One of his own. It had been borrowed for the occasion. Ever hear of anyone borrowing a gun from Graham?"

"I think . . ." She stopped.

"Go on," Bill urged.

"It isn't fair to ask me such a question at a time like this. Any answer I give you will only make you suspicious of a person who is probably innocent."

"You'll have to tell us now," Bill said.

"Well, Claude Stevens is a hunter and he borrowed one of Henry's guns when the deer season opened."

"A rifle?" Bill asked.

"Yes. We were at a party when Claude asked to borrow it."

As they drove toward the Stevenses' house Bill asked, "What do you make of that dame?"

"I don't. I'd like to know just what is on her mind, what she knows, why she looks at me as she does. I'm sure she's keeping something back, but what it is we can't tell."

"Sure she is. I don't think she was too reluctant to keep back the news about Stevens and the borrowed rifle either."

"She's too smart and too worried. What do you suppose Stevens is doing?" Percy asked as he indicated smoke ahead of them.

A thick white cloud of smoke hovered about the Stevens house. Claude was running about the vacant lot next to his house, yelling like a madman, stamping out flaming clumps of grass with his feet, shouting for Nancy to turn on the hose, crying for help because the fire was getting out of hand.

Nancy finally managed to screw on the loosened nozzle. The water spouted free. Bill took the hose and ran with it toward a pile of tumbleweed which had started to blaze furiously. The blaze was rolling toward the windbreak of eucalyptus trees at the back of the property. Nancy joined her screams with Claude's as she whacked at blazing clumps with a bamboo rake.

When the fire was at last under control Claude was disheveled and grimy. His eyes were like cinder marks in a burned blanket. "That rescue of yours deserves a drink," he said as Bill continued to wet down the edges of the burned area.

"We're more interested in the slacks you wore last night," Bill said.

"Come up to the house. Hey, Nancy!" he called. "They

want those pants I wore last night."

"Then they'll have to go to the cleaners for them," she said crisply. "They're not here." She went into the house, slamming the screen door behind her.

Claude shrugged.

"You'd better get them," Bill advised.

"I'll get that drink first if it's all right with you," Claude grinned.

As he crossed the patio his shoes left shiny resinous prints on the brick.

"What's the matter with your shoes?" Bill called after him.

"Must have been too hot for them out there," Claude said, looking at his feet. "I didn't know this stuff would melt."

"Most rubber will in heat, you know," Percy said.

"That's right, I suppose it will."

"While we're on the subject of shoes," Bill said, "we'd like to see the ones you wore last night."

"Here they are. I might as well leave them out here any-how. Nancy will give me hell if I track up the house." He bent down, untied the laces and stepped out of the shoes. "Be back in a minute," he promised and disappeared through the service door.

Bill picked up the shoes and looked at the crepe soles. "As smooth as a . . ."

"Billiard ball," Percy added.

"Yeah. The surface has been cooked right off them. Beats me. What goes on? He sends his pants away and spoils his shoes. What is he hiding?"

"I'm beginning to smell the well-known rat," Percy said. "Let's go up to Hewing's."

"Aren't we going to ask him about his guns?" Bill objected.

"What do you think?"

"The same as you—or do I? Hell, I'm beginning to talk like Fanny."

"Fanny is on my mind. I seem to sense her fine hand in all of this. Come on!"

They were leaving by the path at the side of the house when Claude called from the window, "Hey! I'm fixing you a drink."

"Forget it," Bill shouted back. "You fixed the shoes, that's enough for one day, and don't forget those pants. I want them in an hour."

A moment later Percy thought he heard Nancy say, "I told you not to do it, those men are not fools."

"Do you think she tipped them off?" Bill asked as he drove toward Hewing's at a speed far exceeding the patriotic limit.

"You mean Fanny. I think in her exuberance she dropped some information. I don't believe it was intended as a tip."

"We'll know when we get to Hewing's," Bill said grimly.

"This is it," Percy said.

A big, good-natured colored maid answered the bell. "Mr. Hewing's gone off," she said. "He ain't here since this morning."

"Where did he go?" Bill asked.

"To the doctor's and he said he was going to hunt for the cleaning man. Mr. Hewing was powerful mad at me 'cause I done put his clothes out for the cleanin' man. I don't know why he should get so mad, 'cause I always send his clothes out."

"Suppose you tell us why you think he was mad," Percy suggested.

"Well, when I come this morning—I jes' come by the day to keep house for him and 'stead of takin' Thursdays I take Saturdays off—he was all right but kind of pale lookin' with his arm done up. I guess his hand hurt him some. I fix his breakfast like I always do and goes 'bout my work while he was eatin' and readin' the paper. I found a mess of clothes in his room. He's a very neat man, but there they was, all rolled up in a bundle and all messed up with blood. I shook 'em out and decided the cleaners was the place to send that stuff. I rolled the coat and the pants in a bundle like I always do and put 'em right there for the cleaner to take away so's he wouldn't bother me. The shirt and tie I jes' burned up with the trash 'cause they were a mess, all ripped and everythin'."

"So he was mad because you destroyed the shirt," Percy said.

"No, suh! It wasn't till the girl come that he got so mad."

"Who? What girl?" Then Bill answered himself.

"Oh—oh, Fanny," he grunted.

"Dat's right, dat's what he called her. Fanny. She come in and had a cup of coffee with him and they talked for a while and then he calls me and asks for his clothes and I tells him they is on the front steps, but when I looks for 'em they's gone and he's mad."

"Just what did he say?" Bill asked.

"He say that we'll likely wind up in jail both of us for objection of justice, and I told him I doesn't object to no justice. I just sent his dirty old clothes to the cleaners. Then he asked me for the shirt and tie and when I tol' him I burned 'em, Lawdy! He was powerful mad, said he'd have to find the cleaner and get the clothes back before the police came. Is you the police?"

"We are," Bill replied.

"Well now you know yourself that I wasn't constitutin' no objection to your justice, don't you?"

Bill nodded. "Sure, I understand how it was."

"Do you remember the color of the clothes?" Percy asked.

She favored him with a wide smile. "Sure do. They was his best blue sport clothes, coat and pants. I remember thinkin' if the cleaner didn't do a good job on them they would look fine on my old man." She chuckled.

"I hope he gets them," Bill said. "Thank you." He went down the path.

"I'll be with you in a minute," Percy called after Bill. The maid was waiting expectantly. "You use the Excelsior Laundry and Cleaners, don't you?" he asked.

"Dat's right."

"Then your old man won't get the clothes." As they climbed into the car he said, "I'd like to lambaste Fanny's fanny. She's given the whole show away. What would you like to do?"

"At the moment a little of the same," Percy replied.

When they reached the center of town Fanny ran out into the road and waved frantically to attract their attention. "For two cents I'd spank her hard," Bill growled as he parked the car.

She ran up to them and reported eagerly. "I've done everything."

"I'll say you have," Bill snapped as he faced her. "Why did you tip them off about their clothes?"

"Tip who off, to what?"

"Marjorie, Stevens and Hewing. Their clothes. Don't you like Mrs. Smead?"

"Sure I like her, I think she's very nice."

"Well, you're doing all you can to cook her goose."

"I haven't done a thing," she pouted. "I was trying to help you, and that's the thanks I get."

"You were supposed to telephone that list of people to tell them about the meeting tonight. You were supposed to say nothing else."

"Well, I thought it over and decided to call on them in person to see how they would act. You can tell more by seeing people when you talk to them than you can by telephoning. You ought to know that because . . ."

"Yeah, I know. So they all get a lot of information out of you."

"I didn't give them any information at all. We talked about the murder and I told them they'd better have their clothes ready for you. I thought I'd save your time. How would I know they were going to send their nasty old clothes away?"

"No, you wouldn't, but you might have considered that possibility. All except Ruth Teale sent their clothes to the cleaners and Stevens ruined his shoes."

"You can get them from the cleaners, can't you?" she asked hopefully.

"No, we can't, because the truck was burned and thanks to you, the evidence is gone."

"Mr. Hewing didn't send his clothes out. His maid did it and he was awful mad."

"We know about that," Bill interrupted.

"It's too bad the truck had an accident, or did it?" she began.

"What do you think?"

"I don't know yet, but there was a reason, wasn't there, and all of them didn't do it, did they? Only one of them could have done it. It does have something to do with the murder, doesn't it? What?"

"The murderer doesn't want us to know that he or she was in contact with that two-by-four, that's what."

She saw Percy's hand. "What happened to you?"

"Burn," he replied shortly.

"Mustn't play with fire. What are we going to do now?"

"If we have any luck you're going home and stay there until seven-thirty," Bill announced.

"I hope you *never* catch the old murderer," she shot back at them.

"If you'll keep out of it we may have a chance," he called after her. He turned to Percy. "I'll have to tell Trenton about this business. What are you going to do?"

"I think I'll look over the school. See you later," Percy promised.

He went into the fitting-room, the sewing-room, the murder room, walked down the halls, studied the stairs. Klip's phrase, "an intimate murder," rang in his ears. He found himself wondering if Klip had said the same thing to Trenton.

He went to the head of the main staircase and stood for a moment where Hewing must have stood before he was tripped. He put his hand out for the rail, realized how easily Hewing's hand had slipped under the guard to be cut by the ornamental steel decoration. He went down slowly and met Hewing as he left the office. "What have you been doing," Hewing asked, "getting ready for tonight?"

"Let's call it reviewing," Percy said.

"Any clues in connection with Graham?"

"Nothing definite, but seemingly enough for Trenton."

"Do you mean that he suspects Gloria of that too?"

"Yes, she was at Graham's house last night."

"She was—when?"

"Just before it happened."

"What was she doing there?"

Percy recounted Gloria's report of her activities the previous night.

"You say she stopped at my house, too. Why?"

"I suppose she was concerned about you." Percy evaded a direct answer.

"Where is she now?"

"At the Grahams'."

"Under arrest?"

"No. She's staying with Mrs. Graham."

"And the police are watching her?"

"Yes. She's right under Trenton's eyes."

"He's trying to hang it on her, isn't he? I knew it last night."

"He believes her guilty."

"And what about you, Master Mind?" Hewing asked with a grin which was supposed to take some of the sting out of the words.

"I'm at a loss. I wish I could help her but I can't."

"Do you mean that you're baffled too?"

"Completely."

"Are you in love with her?" Hewing asked.

"No. We're just friends."

"Do you think she's trying to protect someone?"

"I doubt it. I think she's as much in the dark as we are, or were last night," he replied.

"What does Trenton hope to get out of this business to-night?"

"I can't imagine nor do I think it will do any good. His mind is made up."

"To arrest Gloria."

"Yes. I wish I could find a clue," Percy said regretfully.

XVIII

PERCY WAS PREOCCUPIED as he walked home. "Are you still mad at me?" a contrite voice asked at his side. It was a woebegone Fanny.

"No," he said.

"Is he?"

"Bill?"

"Uh huh."

"He's annoyed, naturally."

"You were too, weren't you?"

"Yes."

"So was I. I was mad at both of you but I'm over that now. It doesn't do any good to get mad or stay mad, does it, and besides, I want to help you."

"I'm afraid of your help. I might as well be frank about it." He smiled at the concern in her face. She was half running to keep in step with him.

"If I have to run I won't be able to talk because I'll be out of breath and if I'm out of breath I won't be able to tell you what I wanted to tell you."

"Is this better?" he asked, slowing down.

"Yes. I'm sorry about the fire in the truck but I don't see that it makes any very real difference. You could find traces of wool and all that sort of thing if it was important but I don't think it is."

"And why not?"

"Maybe you should switch to Twitchell," she suggested.

"Why?"

"Because I gave the Twitchells' maid a lift this morning. She had a bulging bundle. The string broke as she got into the car and one of the things she had was a pair of blue tweed slacks. They were dark blue. She said Mr. Twitchell had told her to get rid of them and she was taking them home to her brother."

He considered that information for a moment. "If Twitchell had killed Smead I hardly think he would have been outside of Smead's house while you were playing detective last night," he said.

"How do we know why he was there or what he was after?" she asked.

"We don't, of course. I happen to know something about Twitchell that you don't. He wouldn't have had time to get down to school and kill Christopher."

"Maybe he was there all the time," she suggested hopefully.

"He was not. He's the only one with a genuine alibi. He received a telephone call at 8.30 while the First Aid class was having recess."

"Oh," she said. "That's too bad because I bought the pants for five dollars. I thought they might be evidence."

Percy laughed for a moment then said, "Perhaps you can make a pair of slacks out of them."

"I wouldn't do it. His wife might recognize them. She called me a hussy last night. What do you think she would say if she recognized me in his pants?"

"I wouldn't know," he said.

"What do you think of Mr. Billings?"

"I'm not altogether sure."

"Neither am I. He's bothered about something. He was nervous as a witch this morning when I went to his office. Mrs. Billings was in there too and when I told them about the rehearsal they were surprised. I just sort of hinted that they'd better wear the clothes they wore last night and the funniest

look went over his face. Of course, it may not mean anything, but he did look guilty and so did she, as if they were
sharing a secret between them. I don't know what their
secret is but I'd look into it if I were you."

"How did Ruth act when you told her?" he asked.

"Like a person who had been expecting bad news and got
it," she answered.

He laughed quietly for a moment. "Did you tell her about
the dress?"

"Sure I did, and she said it was dirty but she'd keep it on
anyway, just to show you that you weren't so smart as you
think."

Percy smiled.

"Did the Stevenses act as if they were expecting bad news?"

"In a way they did but they already had it."

"What do you mean?"

"They were trying to get out from under a hangover. He
said he'd been drinking dog hair all morning, but it was
stronger than that. He'd had enough to make another dog.
I didn't stay there on account of the atmosphere."

"Did they resent you?"

"Oh, no! They treated me all right. They were in a fighting mood. She said he had gotten them into more trouble. He
was cranky and told her to sing another tune. She asked him
if he would like the "Prisoner's Song." They just kept at each
other that way about the clothes and all. It didn't make sense,
really it didn't. Does it make sense to you?"

"No."

"Would you have any reason to want to kill Christopher?"
Fanny asked.

"Good Lord! No!"

"That's what I told Ruth when she started talking in circles
about the one person who had opportunity, motive and police

protection. She couldn't mean anyone else, could she?"

"I suppose not. What did Ruth say?"

"That you were a friend of Gloria's, maybe more for all we know, and that you were found beside the body."

"Did she suggest that I hit myself over the head?"

"She didn't say anything about that because I didn't ask her."

"This is where I turn off," he said as they came to a fork in the road.

"You could come up to my house for dinner," she invited.

"You're not thinking that the way to a man's heart is through his stomach, are you?" he smiled.

"Gracious, no! Not to your heart. You're practically an old man, aren't you? That sounds terrible, doesn't it, but you know what I mean. I'm going on nineteen and you must be, well you ought to be thirty-five or more. Do you want to come with me, now that you know about the difference in our ages?"

"Thank you, no," he said. "I think I'll go home, rest my old bones for a while, have some milk and crackers and—."

"Oh, you're not that old. Well, see you in school."

Bill called for Percy shortly after seven. "You were right about the gun, on all counts," he said. "It fired the shots at your door and it is the same gun which killed Graham."

"Trenton turn up anything new?" Percy asked.

"No."

"Do you suppose Trenton would let me take over after he has his little check-up?"

"I don't know. What's the idea?"

"It hasn't jelled yet. Fanny put it in my mind."

"No wonder it hasn't jelled. Want to talk about it?"

"I'd rather not. Do what you can with Trenton, will you?"

Trenton was at the school when they arrived. He was busy giving Gloria instructions, warning her to do everything exactly as it had been done the night before.

"Who will be Christopher?" she asked.

"One of my men. Dunning," he called. "Be Smead for to-night."

"I'm not keen about it," Bill objected, but Trenton waved away his protest.

The teams went to the cafeteria. Trenton had four extra men with him to act as observers. The victims took their places on the stretchers.

"This team finished their work first." Gloria indicated Percy's group.

"Get going on the transportation then," Trenton ordered brusquely.

Percy and his group tried to duplicate their actions of the night before. When he opened the door to the fitting-room Marjorie was there waiting. She was fully clothed and winked at him. He winked back, closing the door, and went on to room 244. They deposited Bill on the floor.

"Has everything been the same as last night?" the police observer wanted to know.

"No. We didn't knock down a piece of two-by-four," Percy admitted.

"I forgot," Ruth put in nervously. "I didn't suppose we would have to do every little thing."

"You didn't knock it down last night," Higgins protested. "I did. You were on the other side of the stretcher."

"I was not," she denied hotly. "I distinctly remember. . . ."

"Higgins is right, Ruth," Percy declared. "You were on the other side."

"Have it your own way," she snapped.

Together they went into the hall. Hewing came up the

stairs and repeated his message of the previous night. When the lights went out they started to scatter.

"Do what you did last night," the police observer commanded, as he covered them with a flashlight. He moved to a post just outside of room 244.

Percy tried to estimate the time he had consumed last night. He met Gloria in the lobby.

"I can't say the things I said last night," she whispered.

"Don't. Just talk about anything for about a minute. Have you seen or heard anything that might help us?"

"No, nothing. This is farcical." Her voice shook. "He'll put me in jail tonight, I know it."

"No, Gloria. Try not to be so fearful." Percy attempted to assure her, then went on gently. "It's about time for you to leave me. Now I must guide an imaginary woman to the telephone booth and come back."

She slipped away in the darkness. He went under the stairs to the booth and returned to hear Hewing call from the top of the steps, "I'm coming down but not in a tumble, I hope."

His feet on the steps counted off seconds until he asked, "Want me on the floor?"

"Yes," Trenton ordered from the darkness.

Step by step they went through their routine. Hewing lay down. Gloria came. They carried Hewing into the auditorium.

"I was in here several minutes with you," Percy said.

"Yes, we talked about Fred's fall and how I'd changed my mind about giving up my job and going with Christopher," Gloria recalled.

"What do you think, Peacock?" Hewing asked anxiously. "Will this nonsense do any good?"

"I don't see how it can," Percy replied.

"But haven't you any idea at all? Haven't you noticed some

slip, some discrepancy? Is there no ray of hope for Gloria?"

"I'm afraid not," Percy answered slowly.

"We'll get you free," Hewing assured Gloria. "Try not to worry."

"I must go now," Percy said.

He met Fanny in the lobby, together they encountered Marjorie, heard her telling the people in the office what she thought of them. Her heart was in it, her words were scornful.

He caught her arm as she left the office door. "Go back to the closet in the sewing-room and turn on the light, please," he whispered.

"But I didn't go back last night," she protested.

"Please," he begged, "and hurry. I'll be up in a minute."

"What are you going to do with her?" Fanny asked.

"Nothing."

"But—"

"Be quiet and don't mention this to anyone."

"I want to go with you."

"No."

"Well, that's like last night anyhow. Good luck!"

On the second floor he went to the fitting-room and groped his way beyond to the sewing-room. In the thick darkness the glow of light shining around the edges of the closet door seemed exceptionally bright. The light Billings had thought he saw from outdoors when he made his second trip to the building and heard that Christopher's throat had been cut. Or *said* he had seen from outdoors. Had Billings—? In any case, whoever had been in this room could not have missed that steady glimmer.

The conclusion was inescapable. "Lord, but I hate this business," Percy muttered to himself as he tapped on the door and whispered cheerfully to Marjorie, "Okay, put it out now." He opened the door and whispered, "Stay here until you hear them taking me down, then go to the lobby via the side stairs."

He groped his way into room 244. "Where did you come from?" the observer demanded.

"Downstairs," he replied and stepped forward.

"I'm here," Bill called from the floor. "How is it going?"

"Fine, as long as your throat hasn't been cut."

"I thought of that lying here in the dark. My blood sort of ran cold when I heard the first person coming through the darkness. I wanted to run. Silly, wasn't it?"

"Not at all. You couldn't tell what the murderer would do."

"Thank God he isn't too literal," Bill breathed.

Percy knelt beside him, "And let's hope I don't get another bash on the head."

"Isn't it time for Fanny to show up? I didn't tell you that I had dinner up at her house. She's a nice kid."

"Very," Percy agreed.

"Here she comes."

"You're supposed to say, 'Hurry, hurry, hurry,'" she called from the door.

"Consider it said and be on your way," Percy replied.

"Here I go," she called.

"It's nearly time for me to faint," Percy said as they heard voices and returning footsteps.

The faint was not necessary, however, for the lights came on suddenly. The observer stood in the door and announced, "Trenton wants you in the auditorium."

"Bill tells me you want to try something," Trenton greeted him just outside the auditorium. "What's on your mind?"

"One or two points which I think will interest you," Percy replied.

"They'd better be good."

"They will be. Let me see your charts for a moment, will you?"

"Here they are, a time sheet for all the people involved. What they did, how long it took them, a check on every movement."

"Umm, very interesting," Percy frowned over the time sheet. "Very interesting!"

"Just what do you mean?" Trenton asked.

"It needs breaking down, doesn't it? The time is shorter than I supposed it would be. As a matter of fact, I put a stop watch on the activity tonight. I honestly tried to do exactly all the things I did last night. I tried to think over all the conversations I had with the various people. Thinking conversation takes almost as much time as actual talk, if you think in words and not ideas."

"So you think we're short in time," Trenton nodded. "Why?"

"Because the murderer did not repeat *his* operations of last night. Rather obvious, isn't it, that there would be a discrepancy?"

"I think you're wrong," Trenton stated flatly.

"And I know you're wrong. Perhaps this time out of two wrong ideas we may get to the right solution. Why don't you let me try?"

"All right, I'll let you have a few minutes."

Two policemen came down the hall struggling with Marjorie, who was giving them a difficult time.

"This dame came sneaking down the back stairs."

"Don't 'dame' me," Marjorie snapped.

"It's all right, Trenton, Miss Blake did a little extra job for me," Percy explained.

Trenton was annoyed but curbed the impulse to show it. Followed by Percy and his men, he strode down the aisle to face the expectant group.

"We won't keep you too long," he promised. "You know

why you are here. I'm turning over the first part of the discussion to Mr. Peacock, who has some ideas."

There was a quickening of interest. Gloria smiled confidently at him, although there were tears in her eyes. Hewing seemed puzzled. Claude Stevens scowled. Ruth bit her lips. Marjorie, still ruffled because of her experience with the policemen, scowled.

"This is not a happy task for me," Percy began. "Many of you are my good friends. We know one another, have lived together for a long time and now, because of this war, we will become increasingly dependent upon one another for the ordinary processes of living. We are faced with a baffling problem, one which must be solved before we, as a community, can take up the normal course of our lives. For our peace of mind, and for the well-being of the innocent, we must find our murderer."

Heads nodded in emphatic agreement and then popped to sudden alertness as he said, "Miss Teale, will you tell us why you hit me over the head last night?"

A gasp escaped from the group. Ruth was dumfounded. Her face paled. She rose slowly, leaned against the seat for support. "I didn't hit you over the head," she denied in a flat voice.

"Then why were you so anxious this evening to say that you had knocked down that piece of two-by-four last night?" he demanded.

"I—"

"You were afraid we would connect the blue wool on that piece of wood with the dress you wore last night. Isn't that true?"

"Yes, it's true," she admitted bitterly. "That's why I deliberately kept the blue dress on this morning after Fanny's visit—to show you that you needn't think you were going to get away with murder. I was afraid and I'm afraid even now. You know why too," she snapped viciously. Her eyes swept over the group, rested on Trenton. "Why are you permitting this Percy Peacock to be so high and mighty? Why has no one suspected him of the crime? I can tell you something about him, about Christopher Smead and Gloria too. Oh, they've been very clever, both of them, but you all know that he and Gloria have been as thick as thieves for a long time. What you don't know, what no one has told you is this: He had an argument with Christopher over the telephone last night before school. Christopher told him he was making a fool of himself over Gloria and that made Mr. Peacock very angry. Why hasn't he told you that? He wouldn't because he thought no one knew it but Christopher. Why was Mr. Peacock at the school last night? He didn't belong there. He attends no classes. Why doesn't he tell you why he came, why he happened to be involved in the case? He knew Christopher was to be the victim and tied for his slaughter. He was ready for the kill. The blackout helped him."

Before he could speak she went on. Her tongue tried to keep pace with her racing thoughts. "I'll tell you what happened. I did go back to that room after my first talk with Christopher and I'll tell you what I saw in the thin ray of a small flashlight. I saw Percy Peacock fumbling at Christopher's throat, I saw him covered with blood, saw him bending forward. Because of what he was doing to Christopher I took that piece of wood and struck him over the head. I was too late. Christopher was beyond help. I started for the lobby but became very ill. I went into the rest room. There I had time to think of all the things that might happen. I knew no one would believe me. In striking him over the head I had involved myself. I was afraid that it would backfire on me, that he and others would try to make it seem that I had killed

Christopher. That is what he has done, what he is doing now. I don't care what happens to me as long as the real murderer is caught—and he is the murderer!"

She sank into her chair and sobbed hysterically.

XIX

WHEN THE EXCITEMENT had died down, when Ruth's sobs were but an echo of her hysteria, Trenton asked with relish, "Well, Peacock, what do you have to say for yourself?"

"Nothing," Percy replied, "except that I don't see how anyone suspected me. I think, however, with Dr. Klip's help and the testimony of Miss Hayes I can satisfy you that I did not cut his throat. Fanny," he called, "how long had I been gone before you came looking for me?"

"I don't know exactly," she answered, "because time seems longer in the dark. I was fidgety and uneasy. We had been talking about ghosts, don't you remember, and you said you were going to see if you could find the ghost and you went up and it was so quiet and all, and I thought that maybe you had found a ghost and you did practically, didn't you?"

Bill whistled softly under his breath when she had finished.

"Now, Dr. Klip. I gather from what Miss Hayes has said that possibly five minutes had passed. It was perhaps two or three minutes later when you arrived on the scene. Can you give us any idea from the condition of Smead's body how long his throat had been cut?"

"Probably fifteen minutes or longer. I wouldn't make a definite statement," Klip replied.

"Which doesn't prove a thing," Ruth put in hotly.

"You feel quite certain that I cut his throat, don't you?" Percy asked Ruth.

"Yes, I do!"

"Will you swear that you did not kill Christopher, that what you have told us of your actions is the truth?"

"I didn't kill him, I swear it," she cried.

"Have you told us the truth about changing your dress?"

"Yes."

"Did you return, attack the janitor and turn off the lights?"

"No."

"Thank you," he said graciously. "I never supposed that you did but I wanted you to deny it. It was a man who did the job on the janitor, a man who was wearing crepe-rubber soles on his shoes, a man who had a definite purpose in mind when he searched Christopher's body."

His audience shifted uneasily.

"Claude Stevens, what did you do with the I.O.U. you took from Smead's wallet last night?" Percy demanded.

"I don't know what you're talking about," Claude shouted. "Because you're trying to crawl out from under yourself, you needn't try to hang it on me."

"What did you do with the I.O.U.?" Percy repeated relentlessly.

"I never had it."

"Then why did you burn the soles of your shoes this afternoon, burn them so that they would be useless to us?"

"I told you, you should tell," Nancy cried out. "Tell them now before they think you killed him."

"Shut up!" Claude bellowed.

"I won't shut up," she shrilled. "If you don't tell, I will! He didn't kill him but when he learned that Christopher was dead he thought about the I.O.U. and was afraid that if it was found on the body the police would suspect him as the murderer. He was doubly worried because he had had an argument with Christopher yesterday afternoon in Billings' office. He was also worried because of the slapping episode."

"Well, Stevens?" Trenton said weightily.

"She's telling you the truth. I was afraid. I did sneak into the school after listening under the window. I struck the janitor and turned off the lights. I took my I.O.U. from Christopher's wallet—but I didn't kill him, I didn't, I tell you."

Trenton looked skeptical, turned toward Percy.

"He's telling the truth," Percy declared. "He didn't kill Smead, neither did Ruth Teale."

"Then who did?" Trenton demanded.

"Just a minute, Trenton. Look along the front row and tell me if you see anything of interest facing you. See the sole of that shoe?" He pointed. Billings' foot thudded to the floor and, for the merest fraction of an instant, Percy thought he saw fear in the dead pan.

One by one the other feet went to the floor. Hewing alone kept his leg nonchalantly crossed. He was leaning forward with absorbed interest.

"You mean the tracks in the Graham kitchen," Trenton said slowly. "I'll be damned."

"I mean that Hewing is the murderer of Smead and Graham."

The amazed reaction of the group was cut by Hewing's derisive laugh. "I'm surprised at you, Peacock." He spoke slowly and deliberately. "I confessed last night because I wanted to save Gloria but you wouldn't believe me. Surely, because you're baffled you're not going to try to make it seem possible that I actually did it?"

"I will prove it," Percy replied, his voice as calm as Hewing's.

"How? May I ask?"

"By a number of things. We will go back a bit. You have been in love with Gloria for a long time. She has given you no real encouragement but you would not give her up. You believed you could *make* her love you. During the recess Gloria told you that she was going to give up teaching, that she was going back to Christopher. You will admit that, will you not?"

"Yes, that's true."

"When we carried Christopher upstairs on the stretcher you were standing in the office door watching us, remember?"

"Yes."

"You heard Fanny ask me where we were taking him and you heard my reply."

"I don't remember that."

"We'll let that pass for the moment. No one but Gloria and the judges of the teams knew to which rooms the victims were to be transported. When the blackout came you dashed upstairs. Our team had just left room 244. You told us to spread the word about the blackout."

"True."

"You knew where Christopher was lying, bound. You made two trips upstairs after that."

"Yes, I told you about them and why I made them."

"On the last trip you did not investigate the sewing-room as you said you had done. If you had you would have seen the glow of light under the closet door. Miss Blake was in there trying to get out of her dress form."

"She couldn't have had a light," Hewing said. "The master switch was off."

"She used the same powerful flashlight tonight that she used last night. I asked her to go up there, turn the light on, and I saw the glow under the door. You too would have seen it if you had gone to the sewing-room as you claim. You didn't. You went directly to room 244 and killed Christopher."

"Ridiculous! You talk of a knife. Was it my knife? How was I to know there would be a knife there?"

"You didn't know, but it was conveniently there. Mar-

jorie had dropped it. You stumbled over it as you went in and
it suddenly struck you that this was a quieter method than
using the gun which you carried," Percy said quietly.

Hewing's surprise betrayed him for an instant but he suggested brashly, "Go on, let's hear the rest of your theory."

"But there was one trouble. Your right hand was covered
with blood, Christopher's blood. Some of it had spattered on
your clothes. You knew the blood would be incriminating
evidence. You had to do something about it. You took that
knife and wiped it clean with a triangular bandage and, holding the knife in the bandage, you cut your own hand."

"What nonsense!"

"Dr. Klip, do you recall the cut on Hewing's hand?"

"Perfectly."

"Did I hear you say today—it was surely a stroke of luck
that I burned my hand and had to visit your office—when you
were dressing Hewing's hand that it was a nice clean cut?"

"You probably did, for it is a very clean cut."

"Was it the type of cut that a person would get from a
ragged, rough-edged piece of sheet metal?"

"No. It was definitely a sharp, clean cut."

"Thank you, doctor."

Percy turned to Hewing. "There were no blood stains on
the metal. You thought fast. You had to have an explanation
for the blood and you had to explain your wound. You decided to tumble downstairs. You fooled us all by saying that
you had been tripped. You were not tripped."

"I told you so," Fanny cried gleefully. "I told you there
wasn't anyone there to trip him."

"You were quite right, Fanny. That's why your teddy
bear was shot."

Curious puzzled glances went from Fanny to Percy but
he made no explanation.

"You should have believed me," she said.

"I apologize for my stupidity last night."

"Your head wasn't right," she suggested kindly.

A slight titter ran around the room.

"I checked the stairs this afternoon and again tonight. Anyone with good night sight would have seen a person, had there been one there to trip you, Hewing."

"So I broke my arm on purpose?" Hewing asked scornfully.

"Last night Dunning was surprised that a tumbler like you should break his arm, remember?" Percy reminded him. "Whether you broke your arm on purpose or not, it did help you and fooled us. You received a great deal of help. Ruth's assault on me, Claude's attack on the janitor, gave you apparently unbreakable alibis."

"It's still rubbish," Hewing scoffed.

"How strong were the pills you gave Hewing, Doctor?" Percy asked.

"They were mild, to ease and quiet the nerves, to give him a chance to sleep."

"Would a man who had taken those pills hear his doorbell if it rang in the middle of the night?"

"In Hewing's nervous condition, I think the slightest noise would have aroused him," Klip replied.

"Do you think he had much rest last night?"

"He didn't look it this morning."

He turned back to Hewing. "You didn't hear Gloria when she stopped at your house. You weren't home. You couldn't hear her. You had been to Fanny's. You had been to Marjorie Blake's. You were afraid of what they might tell. You came to my house and saw Marjorie with me. You tried to kill us both and failed. You had another problem on your hands then, the gun.

"You were afraid the bullets might be traced to the pistol. You decided to return it to its rightful owner, but in order to be safe, you had to kill Henry because he alone knew that you had had it. You didn't expect to find him awake. That was rather a help to you. You killed him in the service porch, then dragged his body out and left it where we found it." He turned to Trenton, "Those threads you found were not from Gloria's bandages but from the gauze on Hewing's arm."

"Who told you?" Trenton asked.

Percy did not reply but went on talking to Hewing. "You thought you were safe until Fanny called on you this morning. You were furious with your maid because she had sent your clothes to the cleaner. You had intended to burn them because they were full of Smead's blood. You didn't want the police to make that discovery, the one thing which might prove your guilt."

"Huh!" Hewing scoffed.

"You knew your clothes would have to be destroyed before the police could get to them. You told Fanny that you would try to find the truck so you could return the clothes to us. You found the truck all right and discovered that it had burned up, probably from a cigarette carelessly thrown by the driver. Luck was with you, Hewing, but not for long."

"You haven't proved a thing," Hewing scoffed.

"Those shoes you are wearing, you were wearing them last night. When you had disposed of Henry's body you returned to the house, crossing the flower beds. There was dew on the ground. You went through the kitchen to Henry's room to replace the gun. If we can prove nothing else we can prove that you were at Graham's last night because we know that the maid scrubbed the kitchen floor after dinner before she left for the night."

That was the one lie Percy told and it had come as a sudden inspiration. It had the desired effect. Hewing jumped to his feet, looked wildly about, would have bolted but found himself entirely hemmed in by police.

"Well, I'll be damned," Bill said. "His confession sure had me fooled last night. I thought it was a grandstand play."

"It was," Percy agreed, "and a good one."

"Would you like to make another confession?" Trenton asked Hewing.

"Are you sure you'll believe me this time?" Hewing asked.

"We don't have to believe you," Trenton replied. "We have proof that you did it, thanks to Peacock."

"I underestimated you, Peacock," Hewing said. "And I forgot about my shoes. I thought of everything else but I couldn't know the floor had been newly scrubbed, could I?"

"Why did you do it, Fred?" Gloria asked. She had been crying.

"Christopher gave me the idea. He had laughed at me before class for being in love with you, said I didn't have a chance, said that dead or alive he could hold you against me. It was a challenge. I don't think I meant to kill him when I went up there. I wanted to reason with him. He wasn't reasonable. He sneered at me, laughed, said what I have just told you, acted that way when I was trying to free him from the splints. My hand hit that knife on the floor. He told me to hurry, and release him. I tried to argue with him. He laughed. I hated him, I wanted him out of my way, so I killed him. Peacock has told you approximately what happened after that." He shrugged. "I gambled and lost. I'm willing to pay."

"Take him away," Trenton ordered.

The handcuffs were snapped on. They started up the aisle with Hewing.

Claude Stevens sighed and slid to the floor in a dead faint. Nancy screamed.

Mrs. Billings waddled across the room. "No wonder he fainted. It must be a relief. Lift up his feet. I'll get my smelling salts."

Gloria was crying.

Ruth Teale said sheepishly, "I owe you an apology, Percy."

"I owe you a vote of thanks," he said. "That crack over the head you gave me nearly ruined our chances of ever discovering the murderer. If you hadn't been so nervously worried about your dress, if you had remained quiet about that stick of wood, I could not have been sure that it was you who hit me. Marjorie's flashlight, the doctor's remark about the clean cut, and the footprints at the Grahams' were the little things which cleared the way back to Hewing."

"Aren't you going to give me any credit at all?" Fanny asked. "I told you there wasn't anybody there to trip Mr. Hewing because I can see in the dark, and that isn't all I can see either." She nodded her head in Gloria's direction.

Bill was sitting beside Gloria doing his best to soothe and quiet her. His voice was low and intimate, his manner protecting.

Gloria looked up at Bill and smiled. He took her arm, helped her out of the seat and started her up the aisle.

"What's she got that I haven't got?" Fanny asked. "Darn it. I gave him such a good supper too." She grinned at Percy. "Well, if that's the way it is, that's the way it is. I'm beginning to think that a young man is apt to be fickle."

"Fanny, stop your gabbing and bring us a glass of water," Mrs. Billings said crisply.

"For drinking or dousing?" Fanny asked before she scampered up the aisle.

"Thank you, Mrs. Billings," Percy said.

"For what?"

"I'm not altogether sure, but I think that something that had never happened to me was about to happen. Good night."

END

www.ingramcontent.com/pod-product-compliance
Lightning Source LLC
Chambersburg PA
CBHW031134260626
47153CB00021B/1472